ONE
MESSAGE
REMAINS

PREMEE MOHAMED

 PSYCHOPOMP

ONE MESSAGE REMAINS

ISBN-13: 979-8-89116-010-1

Published by Psychopomp
psychopomp.com

Cataloging-in-Publication Data
Names: Mohamed, Premee, author.
Title: One Message Remains
Description: Woodbury, VT : Psychopomp [2025]
Identifiers: ISBN: 9798891160101 (paperback)
Subjects: LCSH: Fantasy fiction. |
BISAC: FICTION / Fantasy / General. |

Cover & interior formatted by Christine M. Scott
clevercrow.com

Cover illustration by John G. Reinhart

TABLE OF CONTENTS

ONE MESSAGE REMAINS

My dearest wife,

Major Lyell Tzajos frowned at his letter, if you could refer to it as such at this stage of development. So far it was just a salutation. And a slightly awkward one, no? At home, he didn't call her "wife" any more than she called him "husband." He crossed it out and wrote below it:

Dear Mariye,

Then he paused again, the pencil-tip resting against the gridded paper of his army-issued notebook. Something in her last letter had angered him, something he wanted to refute at once, but he had mistakenly left the letter back at headquarters six weeks ago. He shifted uncomfortably on the low equipment chest on which he had unwisely chosen to rest, the cold metal draining heat through his trousers, and stared out at the horizon, or where he thought it probably was; here, it was rarely a line dividing earth and sky, only a place where the fog changed color, like partly wetted paper. Ah! Now he remembered.

He wrote,

> *Of course our mission is not a punishment. Where did you get such a scurrilous idea, and why are you repeating it to me like any town gossip? If it was from the Tribune, then I order you to cancel our subscription to that rag at once. I have had <u>enough</u> of letting you "sweet-talk" me into allowing you to keep it. It shows great disrespect. Our mission happens to be an <u>honor</u>. For the sake of accuracy, allow me to clarify what we are doing here and wh*

"'Scuse me, sir."

Tzajos looked up as his second-in-command, Captain Yather, approached in a kind of sidewise scuttle, like a land crab. Yather was a tall man at home and conspicuously tall here, and had taken to various contortions to seem less threatening. Tzajos reminded himself to have a word with the man later: it was unseemly, even if it was not technically against regulations. "Captain?"

"We got a, uh. You know. Locals."

Tzajos accepted the pair of field glasses Yather handed him: yes, not more than fifty or so yards to the northeast of their site, a handful of figures in the fog. "Well," he said uneasily, "I suppose there's no law against *watching* us work."

"Nossir," said Yather.

Tzajos hated this kind of thing, hated even more that his hands were trembling as he returned the field glasses. The men were watching him now, all paused in their work, seeing what he would do. Their eyes on him like hands, reminding him of the unfriendly nudges and shoves he'd gotten last time he was in a pub in the capital, spilling his drink. *Oh ho ho, let's see what the pencil-pushing little prig does now.* Tzajos was a compact, tidy-looking man, well within the acceptable height and weight range for the draft, but something about him made him seem not only small but cropped, as if he had been trimmed to reduce even what meager portion nature had given him. The men often appended *little* to the jibes they thought he could not hear.

He tightened his jaw. "However," he added, "one may infer they've been approaching us for some time, unseen. Therefore perhaps with hostile intent."

"Could be, sir."

"Take a couple of men and frighten them off, captain," he said loudly. He did not dare look around to see the faces of the men; even the suspicion that they were laughing made him blush, which would be painfully conspicuous with his fair skin and hair. "Go on. Use the flares. Or no. Wait. Live ammunition, if you please."

Yather hesitated, then turned to the young soldiers behind them. "All right, you lot, tools down a mo.' Volunteers? Yes, you'll do. With me."

In mere moments, the three men were immersed in the fog, invisible, their footsteps silent on the grass. Tzajos held his breath and hated himself for it: a silly little man, yes, just as they muttered under their breaths, a silly little posh prig with a la-dee-dah accent and a fussy little mustache who had no right to command this mission... He swallowed, flinched, rammed his hands into his trouser pockets as the flares went off, even though he had approved their use.

A crackling roar from the tiny cartridges, magnified and deepened by the fog. A sphere of pink light. The sound of unseen birds winging away. Then faint shouting, and a couple of small-caliber reports. As always, even the sound of the guns made him feel light-headed. He had no idea how he had survived basic training. How long ago it seemed, five years, the start of the war...

Yather and the two privates returned, squelching across the wet turf. "Drove 'em off, sir. No contact. Had the men fire into the air."

"Thank you, Yather." Tzajos raised his voice for the benefit of the others and added, "No harm done if you had though, eh? Dragonish hides as they've all got?"

No one laughed. Tzajos had heard the men make a variation on this joke a thousand times since they'd started; what had he gotten wrong? He swallowed again, hearing his throat click, and added, "Right. Well. Are we...are we ready to proceed again?"

"Mule's workin' again, sir," someone called—one of the mechanics, spackled in grey mud from head to toe, like a gargoyle. The Mule was what the men called their temperamental pneumatic excavator, since enlisted men (Tzajos had begun to realize) gave a nickname to everything from their mess kits to local landmarks. He, meanwhile, stubbornly continued to refer to it using its asset name.

"Very well," Tzajos said over the rattling hiss of the engine getting up to steam. "Permission to resume." That was the mission plan, that kept things organized and efficient, he had drawn it up himself: one sector opened up as the next was recovered, followed by closure concomitant with the next sector being opened up. No idleness, every man-hour accounted for! They were not in this foreign land on holiday!

Tzajos looked around for the Teleplasm Recovery Unit in its heavy brass case, finally locating it next to the excavator, also covered in mud. "Private! What is the meaning of this?"

The mechanic wriggled out of the coal compartment and made an effort to clean his face somewhat. "Sir?"

"The recovery unit."

"Oh! Well, she were acting up last night, sir, so I gave 'er a check this morning—"

"What was the issue specifically? Did you complete the formal inspection checklist?"

The mechanic frowned, mud flaking from his forehead. "No sir, on account of that's an official task of which I myself was not assigned to do."

"Then why did you 'give it a check,' private?"

"She...she were acting up. Can't have things acting up."

Tzajos picked up the case, grimacing at the filthy handle. He would never understand these men, never. What was the compulsion to simply *fiddle about* with things unless you had official orders? You could be written up for that. He himself tried to model ideal military behavior, never as much as touching the equipment unless it was part of the mission plan.

Somehow the fog had grown even thicker; visibility was down to a few paces. Tzajos slid his boots rather than walking as he neared the excavation, letting it appear gradually, its edges claggy, grey, more like cement than soil. Next to it lay the cut turf they had rolled up like a medieval manuscript, ornamented appropriately with wildflowers, sprouting herbs, the grasping white fingers of roots. Remarkable, really. The tenacity. How anything *managed* to grow in this stuff. Bit like the people.

Tzajos set the unit down carefully, grateful to be relieved of the burden, grateful also that over a month and a half of constantly hauling it around (as the commanding officer, he was the only one approved to use it) he no longer grunted or whimpered when lifting it. He did not feel materially stronger, but something had been quietly compensating in his arms or back, and he thanked it. Bone gleamed out of the muck, first revealed then polished by the Mule's pressurized hydro-vacuum hoses. A successful find; but as this corroborated the official sector map he had been using, he felt vindicated rather than gratified to see it confirmed.

"Mark it," he said to Yather. The captain dug the map out of his satchel and squatted on his haunches, head still level with Tzajos's ribcage, and glanced around for the bright red flags of their distance markers. Very good; Tzajos had stressed upon all the men the importance of those markers, of placing them deeply in the turf, and it seemed to have sunk in at last. You had to be precise. No sense doing half a job.

"Marked," Yather said, showing his notebook page.

"Thank you. Right. Distance, please." Tzajos stooped next to the excavation, opened the case, activated the device, and waited as the internal engine hummed up to pressure. It sounded all right; what had the private been talking about? Perhaps slightly rougher than usual, but it was barely perceptible and might easily have been a result of sitting there in the mud, instead of its elevated leather frame. Hmm. Maybe he *should* write the man up, after all. It would be a lesson to the rest of them.

When the indicator needle hovered at fifty pounds per square inch, Tzajos flipped the switch and held the funnel steady as whatever remained of the dead men's teleplasm rose from the bones, entering the collector receptacle in a thin violet fog. Strange to look at it, see it the same as our own, isn't it. You'd think it would look different. But then, so many peoples of the world. Maybe not enough colors to cover them all. Or not able to perceive the difference...well, the army tested you for color vision before you could join, and—

Tzajos did not hear the bang, only the echoes of it returning to him muffled and soft in the fog, and he did not see the flash, only feel its dazzling imprint as he blinked again and again, unable to stop his eyes trying to recover their vision. Gradually he became aware of Yather pulling him up, calling his name.

"I'm all right, I... What happened?"

"Not sure, sir. Sounded like one of them stunners went off, except smaller. Like a cherry-bomb."

Tzajos rubbed his left ear, which was still ringing. Fortunately he had dropped the recovery unit at the edge of the excavation instead of into it; the unit did not seem to have sustained any damage, and indeed was still running. He picked it up, wary of a repeat of whatever had happened, but the indicators appeared normal and even the engine sounded normal now. Perhaps it had not been the unit at all; perhaps he had simply had a funny turn and blamed it on the thing.

Right on schedule, the status light turned from amber to green, and it unceremoniously jettisoned the sealed cube of teleplasm from the nacelle, which Tzajos was used to by now, catching it deftly before it fell into the hole. He labelled it with a grease-pencil and put it in his satchel, hearing the celluloid edges clunk dully against the others collected this morning before the Mule had broken down. A bag full of achievements, each carrying him closer to the end of the mission, to promotion, celebration, veneration.

"Effects, sir," said one of the privates inside the hole, handing Tzajos a black bag. He accepted the cold, sodden package between thumb and forefinger, and murmured something about getting back on schedule.

With practiced distaste, he ungimmicked the complicated ties and folds, opening the thick oiled leather to reveal a mass of papers barely damp on their edges. This too no longer surprised him; nearly all of the dead soldiers had been buried with journals, letters, books, pocket watches, and rings in bags like this—things that any reasonable man would have insisted be sent to their families postmortem. Instead the dead clutched them tight, in graves so shallow that any passing wildlife could easily root them up and scatter their remains. A beastly practice in every definition, Tzajos thought. Like dogs burying a bone six inches down, uncaring of what happens to it next, because dogs don't know what a future is or how to think about it. At least they hadn't been in mass graves, as everyone had expected.

At any rate, as the commanding officer, it was his responsibility to ensure everything was read, cataloged, preserved, and transported back to headquarters in order to correctly match physical and teleplasmic remains to names of the dead. The burden of superiority!

He opened the topmost item, a thin green notebook like the kind given to schoolchildren, and glanced at the first line in its clumsily curled printing—*They say the havuvara have weapons that the world has never even*

HEARD of—then put it back in the bag. More efficient to batch everything together and read it all at once after the day's work was done, as he usually did.

As per regulations, the men worked until sunset, then retired to the steam-tracks for the last tasks of the day, wearily traversing the ladders bolted between the high rubber treads, occasionally cursing or slipping if exposed anatomy touched the hot metal of the engine or steam-lines. Twilight dyed the grey soil a vivid blue. Cubes: arranged in spark-proof wooden crates. Bones and teeth: bagged in sanitary cellulose sacks. Sacks: labeled in three locations, stored in individual waterproofed card-board boxes. Boxes: labeled on all sides.

"The least we can do for the poor beggars is a proper job," Tzajos said to Yather as they finally trudged up the steps of their transport and settled into the damp, sooty cab. "The very least. I always think—not even at the *political* level. But as *humans*. The least we can do is offer assistance to a defeated enemy." From the back, just audible through the grate separating the compartments, he could faintly hear the men talking, singing, some already snoring. Was the interpreter in this one?

Tzajos squirmed around in his seat as Yather started the engine, raising his voice over the noise. "Calamuk! Are you back there?"

The interpreter climbed over the other men and brought his face to the metal grate: a thin face, ruddy brown, dark blue eyes encircled by matching dark blue smears of exhaustion. "Sir."

Tzajos said, "What does *havuvara* mean, lieutenant?"

Was that the shadow of the grate flickering across the man's eyes, or something else? After a moment he said, "Who said it?"

"A dead soldier. In his journal."

Again the pause. "A kind of insect, unwanted. You would say roach or cockroach."

"I see." Tzajos dismissed the man and drummed his fingers on the console, raising the faint odor of wet leather. He prided himself on his mastery of the enemy tongue—Dastian was a devil of a language compared to the ones he had studied in university. Not so much the vocabulary, needing only rote memorization, but the way everything shifted depending on the speaker. An unattributed word had, essentially, no useful meaning. What on Earth kind of language was that? In his own tongue if you said "roach" it always meant "roach," no matter who said it or when, dead or alive, no matter whether it was printed in a book or scribbled on a wall.

Anyway. Let the dead boy call them whatever he wanted. Heavens knew armies the world over had nasty terms for the enemy, always had, always would. He was dead, virtually all the Dastian soldiers were dead, Eastern Seudast was crushed, pacified, and occupied, end of story. Soon enough their language would die too, replaced by Treotan. Once the schools were up and running, once you trained the kids to be properly ashamed of speaking the tongue of the defeated, to tell their families not to speak it at home...might take a few generations. What of it?

What happened next to this place really did not matter to Tzajos. He would be far from here, lauded for this mission of mercy, the unexpected kindness of the triumphant nation showing that they really did care—that they had come to recover all these remains and treat them with proper respect, and give them back to the Dastians instead of leaving them to languish in battlefields far from their homes. And he would be promoted, commended... That was one thing. The extra money, the stripes and dots, those were one thing. He would be *respected*. That was the other thing. That mattered. When he was back in civilization again, instead of in this raw and weeping wound of a land, he would be treated with proper respect. For once in his life. For once in his entire life.

How many of the men had seen him faint near the hole today? He hoped only a few. At any rate, at least it wasn't another equipment malfunction; the Recovery Unit had worked flawlessly for the rest of the day. They had been plagued by difficulties for the entire mission so far, and there were still six months (six months!) to go. The unit of twenty included two mechanics; perhaps he should have requested more before setting out.

As if reading his mind, Yather said, "Might need to allot an extra day at the next village, sir, if it'll fit in the schedule. Ruran tells me there's so much mud up in the works that the only way to get the Mule and some of the steam-tracks workin' properly again is to disassemble the engine compartments and suchlike, clean everything out, and put it back together."

"A day? I suppose we could manage a single day. I did build some contingency time into the schedule."

"It would be much appreciated, sir."

"Ruran... He's the bigger one, yes? With the red hair?"

"No, sir." Yather's tone was only lightly reproachful. "That's the other mechanic. Garawe. I can see how you'd get them mixed up, though, as they're usually workin' on the same thing. Ruran was the one you were talking to this morning."

"Of course." Tzajos blushed again, glad no one could see it now. He and Yather had met at headquarters six weeks ago, just before mobilization, and yet the captain had instantly gotten to know all the men, while Tzajos, who had reviewed the detailed personnel folders a half-dozen times, still could not keep them straight. He hated that about himself because it was something he could not change no matter how diligently he studied. And when was the last time study had not solved one of his problems?

Tzajos glared out the windscreen at the landscape bumping and rattling around them, minimally illuminated in pale gold by the steam-track's headlamps. Grass, flowers, bushes, mile after mile of undulating, undeveloped meadow. He glanced into the rear-view mirror to gauge the dark and wavering track of mud they'd left behind them. Well. It was spring; that would grow over in no time.

He was looking forward to summer, and drier conditions. The equipment they'd brought was all meant for civilization, which was to say back home in Treotan, which was to say paved roads, or at least dry soil. What a lot of setbacks they'd had so far! Broken-down machinery, minor injuries, prying locals, one brief but disastrous bout of food poisoning, incorrectly stowed equipment meaning a day-long backtrack to a previous site, fuel shortages, inoperative cabling stations, biting flies...nothing really worth writing home about, he admitted, but they simply never *stopped*. And look at this: one of the sodding little local lizards, blue and brown, right here in the cab! No doubt preparing to empty its parasite-infested bowels onto Tzajos's shoulder. He glared at it; it glared back.

On the other hand, the successful overcoming of these setbacks would look good in his official report and (if he was being honest) the book he intended to find a publisher for when he returned. Their mission was noble, and only made *more* noble by these travails, that was the spin he'd put on it. It would sell like hotcakes. And it would show people back home what it was really like out here in the theater of war, never mind that he had not been in active combat. He'd sort that out later. A few evocative details would suffice.

One feels as if one were on another planet, he imagined himself writing. In a nicely-appointed office in a house—not the sitting room back in his pokey little flat—on one of those new-fangled type-writers that cost six months pay. It must be bright red enamel with gold trim, like the demonstration machine that the pretty girl typed on at the stationery shop to draw buyers in.

There are no streets and no street lamps, no sign-posts, no bridges, dykes, houses, inns, barns, fences, in short, not a single sign of civilization for dozens of miles at a time. One night we traveled quite literally from dusk till dawn (they had, too; since there was nowhere to stop, they simply had to switch out drivers every few hours) *without seeing anything created by human intelligence. Only grass and sky.* Nine hours of pitch darkness emphasized rather than diminished by the wobbling orbs of the head-lamps in the infernal, neverending mist, and he thought they were all going to go mad before morning. He, for one, nearly cheered when he finally saw the tiny specks of candlelight in the distance showing that the village on their map was real, did exist, was not a phantom created by some bored cartographer back home, and was only a few hundred miles off from where it was supposed to be.

Or a phantom created by the villagers themselves, an illusion... Tzajos was a modern man. He did not believe in magic; he knew that there had been a period in the long-ago past when people of his nation and others took it seriously, because they had no other explanation for natural phenomena. In Treotan, magic was supposed to be a gift of the gods; here in Seudast it was said to come from the land itself, like a mineral dissolved in the soil or something. Either way, it was just an idea. Not real. But after that terrible night if you had told him that magic was real, and that the Dastians practiced it, and were using it to hoodwink him and his men, he would certainly have believed it, and with his whole heart.

He shuddered, then comforted himself by imagining the writing, again on the imaginary type-writer, his manicured fingers (yes, he must get a manicure when he got back—the *moment* he got back) on the heavy, curved keys. *War*, this future Tzajos typed, *has a way of changing the beliefs and morals of weak-minded men. However, those of a more upright and circumspect bent, such as officers, are aware of this effect, and make every effort to combat it in themselves and in the men they command.*

Such as officers? Such as *myself*. Well, never mind. The book had to wait till he got back and could tell the full story of the mission, start to finish.

Tonight, the village in which they were scheduled to lodge roughly corresponded to the correct distance on the map (thank the gods), and it rose modestly out of the fog on the highest point around, a hill perhaps ten or twelve feet above the endless grass flatlands. Tzajos exhaled slowly, relieved. Three hours of driving after sundown, let's see... He compared the map, the memorized grids in his head, the man-hours, the setbacks. Surely they could afford one or even two extra days here—save all that time out in the field struggling with the equipment. And the men would love him for it.

It took a long time to find someplace to park all the machinery; Tzajos reassigned a few men to drive and spot one another, and he took Yather and Calamuk the interpreter to search out a post office, or even better a cabling station. He was bone-tired, bone-chilled, but protocol dictated that the commanding officer establish communications, and he never disobeyed protocol. The trio trudged through the darkened village, hunting for the few lighted windows in the little stone houses, or even sensible-looking pedestrians, of which there were none at this time of night.

The moon reflected eerily now and then in the eyes of passing cats. Or perhaps they were the foxes—there was a peculiar species here, very small, smaller than some cats in fact, with lilac grey fur and a wavering, human-sounding cry. Tzajos was determined to bring back a lilac fox coat for his wife when he returned. Must buy that last thing, though. Very last minute. Can't have the men carting it around. Optics.

The crack of their hobnailed boots on the flagstones was the only sound as they walked, aside from the distant rumble and occasional alarmed shout of the men back at the lodging-house parking the vehicles. It was a typical village for the region—eight or ten cross streets each way, the barest minimum of civilization needed to service the surrounding farmland. There would be a couple of mills, bakers, blacksmiths, butchers, and usually a temple, although those were all supposed to be repurposed into Treotan government offices by now. Still, it was a slow process, the diffusion of occupation, and perhaps it hadn't reached this far—and if not, then someone would be up at the temple, because their faith, or something, dictated that a flame had to burn there at all times.

"There we are, sir," said Yather, pointing. Tzajos led them up the road, picking his way around the piles of horse dung black in the silver moonlight, and knocked perfunctorily at the arched stone door before letting himself in.

It was a little warmer inside, but not much; the guarded flame burned in a small stone pot set on a carved stone altar no larger than a child's school desk. Behind it sat the night priestess, staring fixedly into the tiny fire and turning a wooden device around and around in her hands. The windows had no glass; cold spring air flowed in like a river, carrying the everpresent fog, the smells of smoke, manure, cut grass, night flowers.

But no matter how slowly and carefully and loudly he asked, the priestess merely stared at him and did not respond. Her face, seamed all over like a baked apple, held an expression of mild confusion that gave Tzajos an inexplicable sense of anxiety. His Dastian *wasn't* that bad. He practiced and studied every night in bed. Forty-five minutes, every single night, without fail. Why was this terrible old woman judging him so?

He turned impatiently to Calamuk, who seemed to be half-hiding behind Yather as if he did not wish for the priestess to see him. "What's Dastian for 'cabling station'?"

"We haven't got a word for it, sir."

"What? Well, how the devil did they coordinate movements during the war?"

"I don't believe they did."

Tzajos shivered, chewing on his lower lip. He didn't like the dimness in here, all that enclosing stone lit only by the single trembling light, he didn't like the empty seats, the silent priestess, the sense that this whole bloody country—and it *wasn't* even a country now! It was a Treotan *province!*—wanted to roll him in its mouth and spit him out, like a cherry pit.

"Why do they even live here?" he asked, generally. "It's the middle of bloody nowhere. They were offered good money to relocate and work on our farms. It was part of the armistice. There's no future here."

Calamuk and Yather did not reply. The priestess gave no indication she had even heard him. "Never mind," Tzajos sighed. "Let's go get a look at this so-called lodging-house. Has to be better than the last one, eh?"

It was, a bit: on the one hand, there were only three rooms for all twenty men plus two officers, and they were unheated, the floorboards bare of coverings, each empty save for four cots; on the other, somewhat making up for this gross insult to hospitality and humanity, the bathhouse was right next door and contained six enormous stone tubs. Since it was the middle of the night, their sleepy landlady informed them, the baths had not been made ready; however, if the gentlemen did not mind a bit of extra labor, they were certainly welcome to fetch water from the well and start the fires themselves. Tzajos made a show of signing for the extra firewood, which after all was not very expensive, and loudly proclaiming that his men were worth it.

Tzajos and Yather bathed last, taking turns so that both commanding officer and second-in-command would not be unavailable at the same time, and crept back to the lodging-house, where the men had doubled up on the cots or made blanket nests on the floor and were all dead asleep. The room was warm and damp both from their exhalations and dozens of the thin, wet towels they had borrowed from the landlady, hung up to dry.

Two cots had been set aside for himself and Yather; Tzajos took the closest to the wall and bade the captain goodnight. In no more than a minute he heard the man snoring away, hard enough to rattle both wooden bedframes.

Draped in his army-issue blanket, Tzajos carefully wound up his torch and activated it on its lowest setting. The bath had eaten up most of the time he had scheduled to write to his wife and update his daily logbook, not to mention complete the catalog of the records excavated today. Letter first, perhaps. Priorities.

to clarify what we are doing here and wh

Holding down the edge of the notebook with the torch in his right hand, he got out his pencil with his left and added the last *y*, then stared into nothingness for a while. Outside, distantly, foxes the color of flowers called to each other with voices like children. "Please! Please, come play!" their barks seemed to say. Horrible creatures. As if the cries of foxes back home were not unsettling enough.

He deliberately added a period after the *y* and paused again. The short hairs on the back of his neck (regulation haircut: hair not permitted to touch the collar of the shirt) were standing up, and with such vigor it was not itchy but actually painful, pulling on the skin. He felt restless, feverish, as well as exhausted, and for a moment he allowed panic to overtake him: Briefings had warned of this very fate! Any number of diseases were on offer in this backward place! Not just the ones that had been defeated in Treotan generations ago but whole new maladies unstudied by science, suffered only by a people as isolated and warlike as this, which civilization could not approach. Something carried by one of their biting flies, perhaps, or the water in the bath, or the air... admittedly, the symptoms didn't seem to line up with anything he'd been briefed on, but maybe they would get worse later. He should write it down.

Instead, he returned to his letter, the pencil scratching across the grid. He would copy it out in fair later, when they found a post office.

> *We have been selected to do what the occupants of Eastern Seudast cannot. You understand that this is a mission of noble charity, due to Eastern Seudast's great poverty, and also in the absence of their former government ordering them to do so. In fact it is an act of compassion unheard of in our time, since the heroes of mythological antiquity supposedly did similar with their fallen foes but these accounts cannot be relied upon.*

That was rather good, he felt. The allusion to antiquity, connecting his mission seamlessly to the long and unblemished line of heroes all the way back to the gods. He wished he could remember names or manners of deaths, or even why they had gone unburied, but never mind. Mariye wouldn't know either, probably.

He rubbed his aching neck. His hands were trembling and hot; he stared at the minute beads of perspiration forming on his palms, then wiped them on his shirt and went on. The heat and humidity in here were too much for the two tiny windows to handle, really. It would be better tomorrow night, after the place had aired out.

He wrote,

> I am sure, as my superiors were sure when they conceived of this mission, that the transport of these soldiers' remains to the Treotan Department of Foreign Collaboration (formerly the War Office) for repatriation to the East Seudast interim government will _greatly_ improve relations with our new territory. My unit has been assigned a hundred and twelve (112) known battle sites to complete and we have completed with great care and detail twelve (12) so far.
>
> I am exceptionally pleased to have received so many of course. I know of commanders who were given fewer than fifty (50). It is a mark of trust in my abilities, and all this at my age of a mere thirty-two (32). As I have repeatedly reminded you, authorities do not request hard work in the absence of competence, because it is counterproductive. The the the the the last night we were ambushed, but it was all right, Gije said "They cannot hear in the fog, stay

calm, don't run around, lie flat stay still," one
man hit but not killed. I think you remember
Ruda who used to work for the blacksmith at
Lurozo. Anyway hit in the leg and

The pencil flew out of his hand, slid under the edge of the blanket, and clattered to the stone floor. Tzajos discovered that he was blinking sharply. Something... sweat running into his eyes. He swiped frantically at his face with the blanket, then crawled out of the cot, attempting to do it quietly. The men snored on, so tired they would not have woken for anything less than an earthquake.

Where was the pencil? He mustn't lose it; it was a gift from his father-in-law, an expensive drafting device with mechanically-advanced leads. There, in the crack between two flagstones. He scrabbled it up in his sweating fingers and gazed longingly at the window. Air, fresh air.

Outside, some of the fog had blown away; he looked up past the low slate roofs and saw isolated stars, the moon a bright blur behind higher clouds. The foxes seemed to have moved on. Ivy rattled against the walls, a noise like someone shushing a baby. *Shhh, shhh. Ssssss.* This was noble too, wasn't it? The great commander, weighed down by responsibility, cannot sleep; he leaves his men to rest and goes outside to ponder...to ponder... What had happened there, with his letter? He hadn't meant to write that, none of it. He had no idea who Gije was, or Ruda. He had never heard of Lurozo.

A rattle of pebbles sounded behind him; he started violently, flattening himself against the wall of the lodging-house, as quiet footsteps seemed to move off in all directions. At least they were not toward him—no, someone was coming. He waited in silence, heart pounding, till someone stepped into the moonlight and stared at him, confused. Only Calamuk the interpreter, barefooted and in his undershirt.

Tzajos peeled himself off the wall. "What are you doing, lieutenant? I...who were those men?"

Calamuk blinked, or Tzajos thought he did; his eyes were so shadowed in the moonlight that he could not quite tell. "I was only coming back from the outhouse," he said, gesturing back over his shoulder at the small stone building set between the lodging-house and the bath house. "I didn't hear anyone else. Everyone is inside."

"I mean...of course. Yes." Tzajos took a deep breath and pressed his sweating hands to the wall behind him, then tried to arrange himself in a more casual posture. There was a certain complicity—no, there must be a different word—well, a connection of some kind, between two people who meet each other in the middle of the night while the rest of the world is asleep, a kind of understanding that to be awake at this time was strange and unusual, even if all that had woken you up was your bladder. "I just wanted to say, lieutenant," he added, in a rush of feeling, "that I really do appreciate your skills on this mission, you know. The general asked me whether I thought I could go it alone with my knowledge of Dastian, and I told him, I said—well sir, if it's possible, I'd like to take an interpreter with me, in case the rural areas have dialects quite different from the cities, and you came *most* strongly recommended. What a help to your people, what an immense...what a..."

He trailed off. His ears burned with embarrassment. There it was again, even if you could not see him turning bright red in the darkness, his talent, or anti-talent, for putting people at ease. Calamuk looked as if he wished to turn sideways and slip into the gap between the stones.

Instead, the interpreter said, "Thank you, sir."

"I shall be sure to consult you as I process the written material we've excavated. I've been meaning to, it's just, you know. Time. Never enough! For the most part I can read the writing, of course, because soldiers print instead of writing in script, but there's...slang, obscenities, abbreviations, um, proper nouns, that sort of thing. Not in my Dastian textbooks, I can tell you that much!"

Calamuk did not move, but Tzajos got the sudden, irrefutable sense that the man was receding from him— flying away into the dark flatlands even as his body remained perfectly still and at ease. "You are reading all of it?" he said softly. "Everything you find?"

"Well, yes. I have to be very sure of identification, you know. The scientists will be counting on my notes. Quite terrible if we were to return mismatched remains to the families, obviously. And it's strange, isn't it, that they...well, I suppose they're young men, not knowing any better. But *burying* all their diaries and letters, instead of making sure they're recovered, how thoughtless and barbaric. Or I don't mean to say barbaric, that's cruel of me. I do apologize. I just mean at an earlier stage of civilization. That's another gift I think we'll be able to give to these people—your people," he added, considerately. "*Preservation* of the written word. Like me, for instance—I keep carbons of all the letters I write not only to headquarters, but to my wife and various other friends. That way, the knowledge isn't lost. You know, until I started studying Seudast I never knew there were 'cultures' who could read and write, who had languages but no libraries?"

Calamuk said, "We also have no graveyards."

Tzajos opened his mouth and closed it again, and while he was trying to think of a response to this non sequitur, Calamuk murmured, "Excuse me, sir," and moved quietly past him and into the lodging house again. As the door opened and shut it sent a gust of humid air into his face like the hot breath of an animal.

———

Tzajos slept badly and dreamt of many enemies. In his usual dreams of persecution his foes had the faces of men he knew—his father-in-law, for instance, with his ferrety, cruel features; or Yather's bland and inoffensive face so far above him; or men he vaguely knew from headquarters, a typist here, a courier there. Tonight they had faces that resembled his own. He woke trembling, pressing his hands inside his clothing to stanch wounds he had not sustained.

Their landlady reappeared, seeming much older in the light of day, swathed in one of the colorful shawls of the region which covered her clothing from shoulder to ankle. Flowers, cats, carts, cows, all rendered in elaborate embroidery, dancing as she moved. The price negotiated for lodging, it seemed, also included a small breakfast— thick clay cups of tea and dense slices of seedy bread, carried in a brass tray by a silent girl who might be the landlady's daughter, with the same exhausted, fragile look and curling black hair.

Tzajos ordered his men to turn it down; they had no need to settle for this foreign peasant food, meant to sustain foreign peasants, when their own rations were both plentiful (this was true; one whole steam-track's cargo compartment was still filled to the ceiling with labeled boxes) *and* scientifically calculated for the caloric needs of a robust Treotan soldier. The lodging-house had nowhere to sit so they spilled out into the street, and ate their rations out of the containers while standing up.

Mist lay in the village like lace, thicker in the low-lying areas; dawn shone through it soft and diffuse, a dull red that slowly became pink, then lavender, then blue. It was still very cold. Frost glittered balefully on grass in every shadow, and they had to break a fresh skin of ice inside the bath- house well to fill their canteens. Tzajos insisted they use the water purification tablets, speaking loudly over the landlady, who protested that the well-water was from the glaciers, filtered through a thousand miles of fine stone, and was the cleanest water any of them would ever drink in their lives.

"They don't know about germ theory here," Tzajos said firmly, addressing the whole unit. "And *you* don't know how deep their wells were dug compared to the latrines. I won't have my men dying of preventable water-borne diseases during this mission."

No one supported him; but no one dissented either, and everyone did as they were told. Tzajos wondered if this was respectful deference to the chain of command, or just the reflexive obedience of enlisted men who believed that the practice of higher-ups making decisions on their behalf was a feature rather than a flaw of enlistment. Either way, he was satisfied with their performance, and was in good spirits as they marched to the outskirts to begin the mechanical work.

As often happened, a few locals—three children and an old man with a leggy white dog—were poking around the vehicles, one child in a tattered blue dress clambering curiously onto the tracks and stretching up to reach the shining brass handle of the cab.

"Hey, no touch! Dangerous!" Yather waved his arm over his head; his hand was empty, but between his holstered sidearm and quick movements, he must have given the impression of brandishing a gun. The other children scattered sparrowlike in seconds; the climber, startled, wobbled backward and fell into the churned turf with a sickening thud.

Tzajos froze, unsure of what to do—run to pick her up? assign one of the men to render aid?—but she got up, shook herself off, and bolted after the others running toward the village.

"I didn't know you spoke Dastian, captain," Tzajos said when his heart finally returned to normal.

"A little, sir," Yather said, visibly pleased. "Only as much as from reading the phrasebook they give us. Most studying I've done in ages, myself." A few of the men chuckled and nodded.

Me, me! I want that! Why do you never give that to me? Tzajos smiled at him. Dignity. Dignity! He was no dog, to scrounge and grovel for their good regard. It wouldn't matter after he came back and got his promotions. "Well, keep it up. It'll be an asset on this mission."

The old man, unfazed by either Yather's cry of warning or the half-dozen foreign soldiers now surrounding him, gazed levelly at Tzajos from the depths of his ragged woolen hood. He looked like Calamuk writ large, as if someone had decided to erect a commemorative statue: tall, big-boned, dark eyes over a prominently sculpted nose and chin, everything chiseled out of red sandstone. He said, "What are you doing here?"

In the village? In the province? In the army? In life, generally? "We are on a mission of charity!" Tzajos said brightly, one of the first Dastian phrases he had learned in his pre-mobilization training. "We are recovering the remains of your men who fell in the war, and returning them to—"

"You are...what? Digging them up? The dead boys?"

"Yes? And recovering also their teleplasm, if any is left." There wasn't an exact translation of *teleplasm* in Dastian, unfortunately; the closest word was *soul*, which Tzajos did not like. The two words meant two different things in a properly run world. Teleplasm was not individual, did not represent a person's internal being, was not by any means "life" remaining after death; it was only a fingerprint left by the dead of their animating principle.

At the old man's grimace of disgust, Tzajos straightened his shoulders and raised his chin, as if it were possible to see the gleam of his insignia in the fog. His written Dastian was miles better than spoken, but he'd rehearsed for this. "They will be returned to the new capital for further processing. And then we'll help the interim government ensure all the men are buried decently, in real graves with marked tombstones, in a location chosen by their next of kin."

The old man was staring at Calamuk, only his jaw moving, the silver of his short beard glinting in the dawn. Tzajos got the impression that the old man wished to speak to the interpreter but felt he could not, since he was in the presence of these foreign soldiers who knew his language. Everything must be communicated openly; no secrets could be transferred.

Good.

"If you don't *mind*," Tzajos said. "We have a great deal of work to do today and it is unsafe for civilians to be near the vehicles during maintenance activities."

When he did not respond, Tzajos turned to Calamuk. "I'm afraid I bungled that," he said in Treotan. "Do you mind? I mean, don't tell him to sod off or anything. Just...it really is unsafe. The steam, the risk of overpressurization or sudden temperature changes, the..."

He hesitated, sensing some difference—everyone had stopped talking. His men had stopped milling about and were all staring in the same direction, their backs to the village, past the parked vehicles to the empty field that lay beyond. *Completely* empty, Tzajos noted with some confusion. What were they looking at? There was nothing but the tall, somewhat ragged grass of last fall, barely moving in the breeze.

He touched Yather's elbow. "Did you see anything, captain? From your, er, extra vantage?"

"I thought..." Yather frowned, and began to take his field glasses from his satchel.

The old man's dog barked once, sharply. As if it were a signal, the world abruptly became noise and fire.

Tzajos had trained with stunt grenades at the start of the war; his body remembered none of his training, and simply lurched clumsily to one side, landing in the thick mud next to a steam-track and then doing a kind of confused paddling motion, as if he could swim to safety. Yather pulled him up no more than a minute later, straining to extract the smaller man from the mud.

"What was it? What happened? Any casualties? Was it an engine?"

Yather compressed his lips and shook his head. "Everyone's fine. Some kind of improvised bomb," he said. "Fertilizer and gunpowder. They stuck them to the back of the transports. Trying to blow off the locks, it seems."

"They? Them? More than *one*? We should—"

"No, the others didn't go off. There was a sort of—fuse thing. It got pulled loose. Maybe by them kids that was horsing around earlier. Lieutenant Quotin's getting them down with a few of the other lads."

"Quotin? He's a sapper?"

"Yes, sir," Yather said, his tone as neutral as possible. "You must be a little rattled from the blast."

"I... Of course. Yes." He felt heavy and cold, as if partly paralyzed—no, it was only the mud, adhered thickly along one side of his uniform. "Captain Yather, you saw something. The men saw something."

"I'm not sure, sir," Yather admitted. "I thought I saw...the grasses moving. It might have only been that old man running off."

"Moving? Moving how?"

"Well, I don't know," Yather said reluctantly. "It didn't look like kids and it didn't look like the wind. If it was men, they might've been watching for when the bombs went off. Come in and finish the job. I don't know. That's *if* they was really there."

Tzajos rubbed his ringing ears, the sound fading, bringing back normal sounds: his men speaking ordinary Treotan, the cautious calls of the birds in the grass. Did attempted, but failed, sabotage count as an act of aggression? If so, he should report it to headquarters as soon as possible. But if it were only the solitary act of bored children, or perhaps local... He had no idea. Bandits, highwaymen, seeking to remove valuables from the transports. It might mean nothing. It probably meant nothing. But it was up to him to decide.

"We don't need all the men to repair the steam-tracks?" Tzajos said. Yather shook his head. "Take a squad back to the village, see if you can find that old man. I want to question him."

"Yes, sir."

Tzajos ordered the men to load and holster their sidearms, and gave them permission to shoot at anything that moved, within reason, while he reconnoitered the area where he thought he had seen them staring.

Gods, this country—this *land*. There was simply nothing out here, nothing. All of Treotan, even the relatively rural area where he had grown up, was crisscrossed with train tracks, paved roads, conveyor belts, tram-lines, cables for cabling stations, fences, canals, the markers of development forming a neat grid on the map. Here, people still rode horses, they had wooden carts like from a children's book, they took ore from their distant mountains in the woven saddlebags of pit ponies. And in the flatlands there was nothing but grass as far as you could see.

He crested a shallow rise, walked down its far side, letting the hip-deep grass brush the mud from his uniform. Then he turned around: See? Precisely what he was talking about. The village was gone, the steam-tracks and his men were gone. He might as well have gone to the moon.

A terrible sense of loneliness and dislocation struck him. If he had been standing behind that transport, he might have been killed! It did not matter how "crude" the bomb was. He would have died here in this far-away land, died thousands and thousands of miles from his home and his wife, whose face he could barely recall.

No, that couldn't be true. Why had he thought that? But he tried to remember her face and was shocked to realize he could not, and then he thought he might weep, or scream, as people do when they are presented with something horrifying. He could not move; he stood alone in the thick grass and forgot why he had come out there. He remembered his childhood, digging in the garden, picking berries, and learning to shear sheep, using the triangular iron blades that attached to the fingers...no. No. That wasn't his childhood. He had never touched a sheep.

His hands snapped out from his sides and clutched at the grass, squeezing tufts of it. It was real. He focused on that. Real, not imagined, a kind of tawny brown, mottled with darker and lighter patches of gold; it still had the smell of the fall, not of spring. He touched something adhered to a strand of grass: Dandelion gone to seed? No, white fur.

As if from an impossible distance he saw himself, a mere dot in the golden landscape—a droplet of deep-green ink, no larger than that—parting the grass and calling a name strange to his mouth, forming lips and tongue around syllables long lost to the past. The old man's dog came to him, wary, amber eyes like an owl. *You are calling for my brother,* the dog said, and placed its silky muzzle under Tzajos's reaching hand. *He is dead.*

He is dead, he is dead these many years. Every scent remembered. Littermate loved then killed by a man who smelled like this. The cloud of them that descended like locusts into the valley. Locusts making tracks of their own since the roads of the people here were made by carts and hooves. Then the burial. *No, do not bring him back to the sight of the sky. Abomination! Desecration! Smell of blasphemy. You do not dare.*

Tzajos returned to himself with a sickening crack, saliva running from his open mouth. The dog leapt back from him at once, racing through the thick grass with the desperate full-body stride of fleeing prey.

For what might have been a full minute Tzajos stared out at the grass, trying to remember where he was, who he was. Mariye's face returned to him easily now; his words were his own again. He watched the running dog, still running, putting as much distance as it could between the two of them. Typical of the area. A little gratitude for his hard work might be appreciated, but instead, they were all acting like he was a thief in the night.

At his feet he saw something glinting against the dirt: a cartridge, flimsy brass, unfired. He had seen hundreds of the emptied ones in the soil of battlefields they had excavated, perhaps thousands. Many of the dead soldiers had been buried with pockets full of cartridges too.

What a waste. He felt that if he fell in a skirmish, his men were practically duty-bound to continue fighting by using whatever equipment he had been carrying. Ammunition didn't grow on trees, after all, and one's own life, to say nothing of the war itself, might hinge on one man with a loaded or unloaded gun at a crucial moment.

So it meant nothing that it was here, certainly. As the grass grew in the fall it must have...pushed it up from its resting place on the soil. Even though this village wasn't on his sector map, since the survivors interviewed to develop the map had given no indications that fighting had taken place here. Even though it was so smooth and clean. As if it had just been dropped.

Tzajos put it in his pocket and kept walking. For a second he felt a bright, strange yearning to walk forever—disappear into this endless, unmapped country—simply because he could. When in his life had he ever been so alone?

But no. Enough silliness. The mission.

———————————

One day only. They would move out in the morning. Tzajos and Yather sat on a stone bench in the back of the empty bath-house, a torch between them. Around it, Tzajos had arranged the bits of detritus he had found in the field: a bit of string, metal shavings, three more unfired cartridges, and a flint-strike lighter.

Yather spent a long time with the lighter, turning it around and around gently and holding it up to his eye. "A peculiar find," he finally pronounced.

"I thought the same." Tzajos sighed, and flipped absently through his notebook, where he had interrupted his unsatisfactory letter to Mariye with a drawing of the area he had been searching, and the approximate distance (paced, if clumsily, through the grass) to the vehicles. "Standard Treotan army issue...everyone said the fighting didn't get this far."

"They did say that," Yather said.

"Who dropped the lighter? Our mad bomber, I suppose."

"Could have been more than one. No sir, I didn't see no men out there," Yather said, holding up his hand to forestall Tzajos's question. "I told you already, I didn't *see* anything for certain in the grass, none of the lads did."

"We shall have to set a watch overnight," Tzajos muttered. The men wouldn't like that. After a long day of manual labor, all anyone wanted to do was eat and sleep. But he thought they wouldn't protest too much. After all, the bombs, crude as they were, could have killed any of them. *Could* have. "We're dealing with rank amateurs," he added, picking up the bit of string. "Quotin said this was part of the fuse he found. They had soaked it in something—mustard-seed oil, he thinks—but not long enough, so that it was uneven, and there were dry patches. Instead of burning swiftly along the length to connect them all, it burnt right through and fell to the ground after the first one went off."

Yather nodded.

"And someone fumbled the loading of their gun. And when they saw they had failed, they ran...and no one in the village claims to know anything." Tzajos paged through his notebook again, re-reading the few sentences he had gotten out of the old man, who had been found easily enough in the village and had made no effort to hide or run. No, he didn't know anything; no, he hadn't seen anything; no, he knew nothing about any kind of explosive; that was something the miner folk might know, hundreds of miles away, but they were all farmers here, no one local knew how to make what he was talking about.

"I suppose it's like any war," Yather said after a minute. "The lighter, I mean, sir. You know how it is, any little trinket or trophy that folks find on the battlefield, they pick it up and see if they can sell it."

"Do they?"

"Saw it last time," Yather said, reminding Tzajos again, painfully, that this was his first war and Yather's third. "Afterwards we was given some leave time in Banotin. Beautiful city, barely touched by the shelling. All the fountains and castles and domes and, you know, what do you call them. Towers and such. So me and some of the lads are in the marketplace looking for lunch and a pint, and what do we see but a lady at a bric-a-brac stall selling Treotan tickets." Yather gestured vaguely at his chest, where his official badge of army registration and identification hung on a chain under his shirt. "They'd gold-plated some of 'em and were hawking them as jewelry, if you can believe it. So my mate Therser is over there pawing through them and shouting out, as he recognized a few names from our unit, and he's yelling at this poor lady about looting the dead, as if she did it personal, an old lady like her. Goodness only knows who sold 'em to her or how many hands they passed through. And she had all sorts of stuff—mess kits and helmets, lighters, belt buckles, army pens and pencils, compasses, field glasses, satchels...doing a right brisk trade, too."

Tzajos nodded. Mariye had wanted to go to Banotin for their honeymoon, but he'd had to quash that idea right away. Too expensive, too far on the trains, too foreign; they'd be pickpocketed, swindled, perhaps kidnapped for ransom, but at a minimum they were guaranteed to spend the entire time in their hotel room with upset tummies, he'd heard all the stories. He'd talked her into a weekend at Cleemage Beach instead.

He said, "Our mad bomber."

"Sir?"

"Nothing. I... Look at this village, Yather. All the young men are dead. It's just old men and women and kids and dogs. They're not...they're not *soldiers*. No matter their personal feelings toward us, they're simply trying to dig a living out of this ridiculous soil. They don't want to fight us. So who does? And are they going to follow us and try it again?"

Yather set his jaw, glinting with blond and grey stubble. "Insurgents, you mean, sir?"

"It has to be. The military of East Seudast doesn't exist any more. It's been wiped out—I mean, there were only a handful of survivors left after the armistice anyway, and the government rounded everybody up and decommissioned the whole army. Such as it was. All the weapons and vehicles turned in, everyone straight to the re-education camps. All they've got left is rocks and pointy sticks. Officially."

"Insurgents! Imagine. Hope there's a cabling station at the next town then," Yather said. "We'll have to tell headquarters if we're officially under fire."

Tzajos twitched involuntarily at the mention of headquarters, sending the cartridges jingling to the stone floor. "No! No. I mean, this is hardly proof of anything. We've just gone down a flimsy rope bridge of conjectures, captain. Look at this." He recovered the cartridges and returned them to the other items. "Imagine showing someone this in a court of law later. We'd be laughed out of the room."

"I suppose so, sir."

"The mission proceeds as planned," Tzajos said firmly. "We're going to finish it in good time, with no missed sectors, with no further incidents, and then we are all going to go home and get our enormous bonuses. And you and I will get our well-deserved promotions. Maybe commendations. It's fine. There's no proof, there's nobody."

"...Sir?"

Tzajos wasn't listening; his gaze had strayed to the roof of the bathhouse, slightly peaked, an octagonal well of darkness the light of the torch could not reach. "There's nobody. Nobody out there. Only us."

———

The one thing any potential hostiles could not do, at any rate, was follow them in the steam-tracks; the convoy moved more slowly here than it would have back home, but still far faster than even the most determined rider and freshest horse. Tzajos looked into the rear-view mirror of the cab for the entire drive to the next sector, all the same. He seemed unable to stop himself. Normally he would spend this time reading the retrieved journals and letters of the dead Dastian soldiers, looking up words in his Treotan-Dastian dictionary (woeful though it was), writing his own letters, or reviewing the regulations book. Now it was dead time, useless. The surveillance did not even assuage his fears, because they were too formless and vague to be good targets.

They drove to the next grid, confirmed coordinates, set up the Mule, the lifters, the cutters, the flags, everyone moving slowly through the milky mist, wary of sinkholes and hidden stones. Tzajos assigned two men to fuel up the Recovery Unit and check its fluid levels and seals;

it was not, he told himself, that he was afraid of it at all. Far from it! Only that fresh eyes might perceive any defects or irregularities that it might be displaying this morning. Complacency, that was the problem. You got too used to things, they became wallpaper, you didn't notice something going wrong.

From somewhere nearby, Tzajos could hear the urgent gurgle of a small stream, but he could see nothing; it was probably less than a dozen paces away. Strange acoustics here. The map had been marked with the symbol for mountains, perfect little grey triangles printed by the Special Cartography Unit back home, but these weren't mountains, not really. Instead the land was perfectly flat except for dozens of impossibly high, round-topped black stones, protruding from the plains at irregular intervals like the blunt teeth of whales. Between them lay no valleys, only grass so level he felt he could roll a ball from one end of the horizon to the other. The turf looked as if it had been cropped by a lawn-mower. Even the numerous flowers embedded in it were low and flat, not like real flowers at all but pictures snipped out of a color magazine.

Tzajos stared up at the black stones, wondering about their strange glassiness. Like volcanic rock, really. And faceted irregularly, like a raw gem before being worked, still breaking along internal fracture lines to form shapes made perfect by physics and geometry rather than a lapidary's training. He had no doubt that some of the broken edges were sharp enough to cut flesh; perhaps at the noon break he would go look at them more closely, maybe get a sample to bring back to headquarters.

He wandered off and found the usual equipment chest to sit on, taking his stationery kit out of his satchel.

From both near and far he heard the rattles and curses as the men loaded the Mule up with fresh coal. The *rug-rug-rug-rug* of the engine sounded as if it were six inches behind his head. Imagine fighting here, trying to use the stones for cover, knowing the Dastians were doing the same, since there was simply nowhere to hide. He wondered whether these stones had been on the list of assets at the start of the war, or if the government of Seudast, which had lied about so much else, had lied about this too. There must be an industrial use for these back home; he did not know what it was, but that was not his job.

He took out a few sheets of good paper from his personal supply, and his fountain pen, and his Dr. Bridges Patented Traveling Inkwell (Guaranteed Nev-R-Spill Or Your Money Returned). While the Mule coughed and snarled and got up to pressure, he carefully copied out the beginning of his letter to Mariye, updating it with the correct number of finished sectors. Much nicer to write on the good paper than the soft onionskin of his official army notebook, which developed holes if you pressed too hard, even with a dull pencil, and gods forbid you try to erase anything.

He added,

> *I hope you are working on the instructional "house-keeping" course I bought you before I left. Or at any rate making productive use of your time while I am away. It occurred to me however that since the course included a great deal of sewing you might find it helpful in your "project" to make new curtains for the flat, as we have been discussing for some*

the havuvara are getting closer, we can hear them move at night. One thing they cannot do is move quiet! Always you hear them. Not just their marossa but they themselves talking too loud & so on. Smell them too ha ha. Still though they have more guns & more men & more everything than we do so it doesn't matter. Everyone knows when you want to grind the world to dust you wear good boots. Sundoman says we cannot win this war and it is unbelievable to me. Why war why us why now. All I know is they showed up and said we belonged to them now and we all had to say. No. Then to fight. My ribs hurt where hit yesterday but getting better (I think). Blood stopped anyway.

Tzajos found himself gasping, as if he had been holding his breath; dark lights danced in front of his eyes. Where had those words come from? Stress, that was it. Sleep deprivation. A shame he had been writing on the good paper. Maybe at some point they'd be in a town large enough to have a stationery shop, and he could buy some more to supplement his dwindling supply.

Really, a minor aberration. How they would laugh about it when he came home! *You and your paper hoard,* Mariye would say. *Like a dragon.* And then he could tease her about her fabrics and trims.

Reaching for reality again he studied the blurry, verdant scene around him: the red flags sprouting like flowers, the first rolls of turf already cut with the spades and peeled away in crisp rectangles from the grey soil, an enormous purple beetle trundling past, as big as a golf-ball. A few of the men, clearly not sufficiently occupied, were eating something illicit, and turned hastily away when they felt his gaze. Probably that local black bread spread with the jarred liver paste that they were always bartering from the locals when they thought the officers weren't looking.

Tzajos was irritated; he'd had occasion to reprimand them about it before (it wasn't sanitary, who knew what diseases they might get, the jars weren't even clean on the outside), but they persisted. Perhaps it was worth writing one or two of them up; they never made an effort to hide the jars, after all. What was that again, an Article 25? Minor misbehavior. Give them a little jolt, get the rest of them in line. They thought he was too mawkish, they thought he was cowed by the bomb incident, that he lived in fear now; he'd show them.

He used the trimmer on his fountain pen lid to neaten up the paper's edge, and began the letter again. The pen: Good. Same one he'd been using faithfully since university. Familiar mottled blue stone of the body, familiar blue-black ink (Shade No. 3) in the reservoir. He hadn't seen ink anywhere for sale since he arrived in this place. People here wrote in pencil. He didn't like that. Pencil was for things you meant to un-say.

Dear Mariye, he wrote slowly, making sure of every letter, as if he were a little boy learning cursive again. *Last night we were ambushed. Tulmar, Chakhan, & Konor were killed. We climbed back to base with the wounded though. Arkni is wounded badly (chest). Don't think he'll survive the night. Strange that the havuvara have mechanical lights & could fight at night. But they don't. We are safe for some hours now. Dark up here.*

Quiet. Arkni is sleeping and I can hear his breath rattle. That is the only sound. But it is good, because it is still a sound. We will have to listen for it.

His hand stiffened into a claw, jerked across the paper so that it tore and the ink splattered from the nib, and then he was patting the thick grass to find it, and then he was screaming, everything cold except for his mouth and nose, which were on fire.

Many hands pulled him from the water, held him up while he coughed and snorted and spat. Where was Yather? Must be in one of the vehicles. Didn't see his commanding officer nearly drown. Nearly...had he? As one, he and the three men who had rescued him turned to look at the water. He had heard it earlier, he had thought it must look much like this, and it did: quite clear, fast, shallow. Lucky, that. If he had stood up, it would have come up to his thighs. Fish shot past like freshly polished spoons.

"Are you all right, sir?" one of the men was asking him—young Vzeath, his face a mass of worry and pimples under the sandy hair.

Tzajos looked at the stream again, quite visible, entirely visible, between its two low beds of rushes, and then back at the equipment chest he'd been sitting on: ten paces away. He could still see his boot prints in the wet grass. Slowly he leaned down again, sending a thin stream of water from his nostrils, and wiped his inky hands on the turf. He *had* heard something, this time he knew for sure; the voice rang with clarity in his head still, like a struck bell echoing, young and eager as the bones that matched it. Walking over bones now. Where was his pen? Walking over bones, cleaning his hands with the grass that fed upon them. Spirits in his satchel, pressed to his back. Had to keep them warm until they could be placed into heated storage compartment. Regulations.

He said, "Help me find my pen, if you don't mind."

The men stared at him for a little too long, but obeyed. "Stress," Tzajos said. "Even though we are not in an active battlefield, gentlemen, stress may still enter our bodies—like parasites in unclean water. The cure? Hard work, the company of good men, restful sleep, and fresh air. And of course," he added, raising his voice slightly as they walked back to the others, "the undeniable positive effects of thinking of our mission of mercy! The honor bestowed upon us to be part of this unit!"

"Yes sir!" said Vzeath; the man next to him chuckled indulgently.

"Go on and laugh," said the third, Oughbell; his voice was mild. "But I'll tell you two something while you're laughing: I got three brothers and we all came here to fight and then we all went home to our mum in one piece. And you know what we did next? We went next door to give our neighbor Mrs. D a lift to the cemetery, because her sons both got kilt. But someone made sure to get the bodies home for her. So she could go see 'em and put some offerings down and sweep the grave and make it look nice. There's lots of mums back home who didn't get that though—who still think their kids might be alive out there. Just missing in action. And until you're suffering with that kind of hope, you can still laugh. Afterwards you can't."

Tzajos swelled with pride, and clapped the boy familiarly on the back, leaving a damp handprint. "That's the spirit," he said. "Always remember what we're doing. An enemy mother is still a mother. She cannot be certain as to the fate of her son—only we can do that.

Only we can put her sorrowful mind at ease. Remember that."

Back at the worksite, he easily hefted the Recovery Unit and laughed off inquiries as to what had happened; half-asleep, fell in, you know how it goes. Certainly shan't do that again! Tonight he would stuff his ears with cotton to block out everybody's snoring and he'd get a jolly good night's sleep. Yather watched him worriedly, but Tzajos did not care; he had diagnosed himself with a case of severe stress due to overcommitment to the cause, and that was curable. There were at least a hundred treatments to try in the *Your Health as an Enlisted Soldier* booklet. Deep breathing, nighttime walks, stretching regimens, word or theater games with one's comrades, starting a "nature journal" with sketches of local plants and insects, writing letters home... Well, the other ones, anyway.

He thought, *They do not want me to write*, and then pushed that away, because it was ridiculous.

He thought, *They do not want me to write my own words. That is more precise*, and then he pushed that away too, deeper.

He thought, *They want me to write something else; they have found an opening and it seems they have a purpose, but what?* and he almost fell into the open excavation, catching himself at the last second. He felt disoriented, his legs still numb as if frozen, even though he was mostly dry now from his dunking in the stream. It was the huge black stones, probably. They were disorienting; they made you feel as if you were the wrong height, so of course you couldn't figure out where your arms or legs were. Drunk, that's what it was. Altitude drunkenness. Proximity to stones drunkenness.

Behind him, Calamuk said softly, "We have not found any remains in that hole yet, sir."

"I know that! I know! I can see the colors of the flags! I was *preparing*."

"You're all right? You're not hurt?"

"It was a very shallow stream, Calamuk." Tzajos laughed, coughed, laughed again. "My mind merely wandered for a moment."

"What were you doing when it happened?"

Tzajos turned and met the eyes of the interpreter, who looked back at him steadily. For the first time Tzajos thought deeply about this interpreter, hired after the armistice, a former enemy soldier whose past he did not know—you were not supposed to think about it if they cleared all the security requirements—who might have fought and killed Treotan soldiers, who might have done it here, right here, where they were standing. He wanted to say, *Where is your standard-issue lighter, lieutenant?* Or *Why do you ask? Do you know something that your commanding officer should also know?*

Tzajos said, "You know what I was doing."

Calamuk's mouth worked, but he said nothing; his normally impassive face seemed to waver between fear and resignation.

"What can be done?" Tzajos whispered suddenly, hoping no one else was listening; it was hard to tell in the fog. "You are about to say *Nothing can be done.* Aren't you? You know something. Is it a sickness? What is it?"

Calamuk straightened, recovered his shovel, moved backward. "I am falling behind my team, sir," he said. "I won't take up any more of your time."

All around them the stones reeled and danced and tilted and spun while staying in the same place. The day wore on. No birds sang.

———————————

They worked at the site for a week, recovering twenty-seven bodies and seeing no one living aside from themselves. Only the great gleaming monoliths made them feel watched, and there was a quiet but general groan when they reached the next location on Tzajos's map and the stones were still there—if anything, more numerous and taller.

"What a strange district," Tzajos remarked to Yather as they drove into the village, this one for some reason wedged claustrophobically between a close-set pair of the colossal black stones, as if a peppercorn misplaced on a table had rolled between two beer bottles. All the houses looked the same as the other villages they had seen—tidy, one-story boxes of grey stone with slate roofs and no front yards, the doors opening right into the street. But they were all in perpetual darkness and none had the usual ivy growing on the walls or flowers at the windows.

At first glance the place seemed abandoned, because it was so dark and no street-lights burned, but as they trundled the convoy onto the wide main road where the enclosing stones opened up a bit, they saw the villagers. Quite quaint, really, the women in their long brilliant shawls, the horses with bells on the tack, the stalls selling vegetables and cheese, and the more enterprising children offering to shine shoes or sharpen knives for a penny.

"Saint Samacuk's Day market," Calamuk said through the grating. "That big flag means vendors will have come from many other villages. If we are short on anything, this might be the only place for miles around to resupply."

"Duly noted, thank you, lieutenant. I'll send a squad," Tzajos said stiffly. He found that he did not wish to speak to the interpreter these days, and he did not like that this was because he no longer knew what would come out of his mouth at an unguarded moment. He needed all his concentration now to keep his guard up. He could not look into the man's eyes without wanting to slap him, or shake him, or scream questions at him; and then he would look quite insane because he had no reason to suspect the interpreter of anything, anything at all. One could not court-martial a man based on a vague and undefined sensation of guilt; there had to be a crime.

At last there was a post office, even if it was a tiny one, and even better, it boasted the prominent, bright blue and gold signage of a Treotan Interim Government office. Tzajos felt a momentary sense of homecoming— all the municipalities in East Seudast were supposed to have their Treotan representative by now, thousands of minor bureaucrats, accountants, engineers, lawyers, academics, veterans, and so on had been mobilized from the capital, but despite all the careful planning it had been a painfully slow process. Seudast was simply too big and too remote and too bizarre; it was like a land out of fairytale. Take this village, for instance.

Tzajos joined the postage queue behind a line of locals clutching unstamped letters in identical blue LOCAL MAIL ONLY envelopes, stalled by an agitated old woman who was trying to browbeat the disbelieving clerk into letting her mail a chicken to her sister in Lurozo without putting it in a box first. The windowless room smelled of fresh paint, harsh carbolic soap, and grilled lamb from the enterprising girl who had set up her sandwich stand near the doorway, clearly planning to capitalize on a captive market.

"I have already bound its legs, what else would I need to do? Where is it going to go? Chickens can't fly away. Look, I have the money, damn you!" the old woman shouted.

Lurozo. Why did that sound familiar? One of those mellifluous Dastian words that resembled an etymologically unrelated one in Treotan, luroz, a popular flowering shrub. Various pinks and reds. If you had a big one your garden would be full of bees and butterflies for half the year. *Lurozo*. The queue wasn't moving. He took out his notebook and turned the thin pages backward from today's bookmark.

Too late he realized his mistake, and then it was happening, his body became someone else's, or perhaps it was still his own, moving the wrong way in time— back to the war, to the moment of death, thousands of deaths, a million on both sides. He heard himself shouting to his men, no, not his men, his friends, boys from his village, he heard himself shouting to Tib, the boy he had loved; the firefight hung around him for a moment ragged and blowsy as a cloud, then solid, real.

He was on the bridge. He must not let the enemy get the bridge—those loathsome invaders with their screaming, belching machines that wanted to chew up the whole country, the whole world. A small stone bridge over a white-water river far below, no different than any other bridge, flashes and pops in the darkness, the sharp smell of cordite reaching him in the cold wind, and his back hurt from falling onto the stone railing but also because he had been shot, he just didn't know it yet, the bullet had not penetrated from his back to his front and he could see no blood, Tib somewhere running, *three years later a little sallow man with pale hair and grey eyes will find this bullet and will find my bones and will find this journal but he will never find an account of tonight because I could not write in my journal because I am dead I am dead I am dead and the enemy is a nightmare who holds the high ground*

Villagers screamed and scattered, throwing themselves flat as Tzajos unholstered his sidearm, got off two shots, turned, saw the dark green uniform running toward him, *you you you*, fired again, and then he was snarling and fighting as bodies piled onto him, pinning him to the stone floor. He heard a voice emerge from his throat very unlike his own, the pure voice of a boy, speaking flawless and unaccented Dastian too fast for him to understand. A woman shrieked very near his head.

Someone yanked the gun from his hand; someone else pinned his arms behind his back. The gunfire in his ears faded, the sound of the night wind, the distant roar of the river far below him, and it was Yather, only Yather, in his agitation shouting a mixture of Dastian and Treotan at the horrified villagers as he dragged his commanding officer outside and into the street.

"Tib," Tzajos croaked, staring up at the confusion of faces—Yather, Calamuk, Garawe, framed by the featureless blackness of the stone behind them and a thin sliver of blue-grey sky. "Did he get away? Where is my list—where is the sector map with the list of names? If he is on there..."

"Who?"

Tzajos clamped his mouth shut. After an awkward silence, Yather let him go and he stood, dusting himself off with stiff movements; his whole body was a mass of bruises. "Where are my letters?"

"I gave 'em to the clerk, sir," said Garawe.

"Ah. Well done. Thank you." He reached for his empty holster and flinched, remembering; all the blood in his body seemed to rush to his stomach and curdle there. "Did I...strike anyone? I certainly remember shooting at...at one of you...I can't understand what..."

"You didn't hit anybody in there, and you missed me by a mile, sir," said Yather.

"My apologies, Yather," said Tzajos, and held his hand out for his pistol.

Yather pressed his lips into a thin line; Tzajos slowly became aware that the four of them stood in the center of a circle of villagers that was rapidly becoming a crowd, and had the crackling, thunderstorm energy of a crowd that was about to become a mob. The sandwich girl was weeping quietly, unhurt as far as he could tell, but gingerly touching a neat round bullethole in the card-board signage of her stand; an older woman approached, embraced her, their shawls mingling and fluttering. Where were the rest of his men? Of course... He had sent everyone to their lodgings to settle in and arrange a watch schedule for the vehicles. He had only meant to nip into the post office for a few minutes before joining them.

Yather said, "My regrets, sir, except this seems to fall, in my judgment, which I suppose might be pretty poor, er, but *seems* to fall under Article 32, which I'd like to stress, sir, is *temporary*, until such time as a medical inquiry can be made..." He trailed off under the heat of Tzajos's disbelieving stare, and added, "I'm not givin' it back, sir, until Rothkard gets a look at you and signs the form, is all."

"Rothkard? The one who puts the bones in the sacks?"

"He's a doctor, sir."

Tzajos felt the crowd closing in, not aggressive, not yet, but curious, hungry to see this crazy man who wore the uniform of the enemy and had come into their village to scream at them in their own tongue and shoot at their post office. They were offended; they were relieved no one had been shot; they might very easily tip from hurt to angry. But just a minute: "Article 32 covers removal of command for reasons of medical disability," he said. "When did you look up which one it was, Yather? Just now, before you disarmed me? After? That was very swift of you. Hmm?"

Yather mumbled something, barely moving his lips.

"What was that?"

"Last night, sir."

It was not a betrayal, Tzajos told himself, though the bitterness in his mouth tasted like any ordinary treachery; it tasted like a long-ago girl telling him there was someone else, it tasted like his father admitting that he wouldn't hire his own son to work at his firm. It wasn't personal. It was a *regulation*.

Calamuk showed his empty hands to the villagers and that seemed to defuse something; they did not disperse at once, but they parted to let Yather lead them out of the circle, through the marketplace, up a set of stone steps, down a road, and into the lodging-house.

"Physically, you're in fine shape, sir," Rothkard said, gesturing for Tzajos to put his shirt back on.

"Thank you," Tzajos said stiffly, gathering the discarded bits of his uniform. "I do notice, however, that you are still looking at the form on the clipboard instead of handing it to my second-in-command, followed by myself, to sign."

Rothkard swallowed, his throat emitting an audible click. The room containing their impromptu medical exam had been a dairy back when the building was the residence of the local warlord; it was very cold and the thick, unglazed tile walls blocked all the sound from the street. More than once during his examination Tzajos had thought he could hear the beating of Yather's heart and Rothkard's heart as well as his own.

"Do you *really* believe I should be *permanently* relieved of command for the rest of the mission?" Tzajos prompted him. "If you do, by all means say so on the form; honesty and transparency will be much lauded in any future legal proceedings."

"It's just...overwork. I'm sure. Stress," Rothkard said. He was a slender, fair-skinned man with dark hair in such profusion that it lapped over his collar even with weekly haircuts, and a similarly luxuriant beard that Tzajos had given up on urging him to shave two or three times a day to keep his stubble below regulation length. He looked like a plant stem too fragile to support its resplendent flower. "It's likely to resolve on its own. It's just, I'm sure you'll agree that if it doesn't, we simply *can't* have you armed. We just dodged not only a local tragedy but, possibly, a re-opening of hostilities on a national level, a violation of the armistice—shooting at unarmed civilians. What if there's a next time? What if you kill a child, or a village elder? Or one of us? After today, can we really say it won't happen again?"

Tzajos couldn't. His shame was incandescent and absolute. They sat in stalemate for what felt like a year before Yather said, "Well, I don't want to run this circus either; the major here's the better chap for it in all respects, and we all know it. Is there some kind of middle ground?"

Rothkard shrugged. "Maybe we don't have to do anything right now," he said after a pause, setting the clipboard aside. "I'll make you up some sleeping pills, my own recipe. It's frightful stuff, but you're guaranteed to sleep. You'll be incapacitated, legally as well as technically, for about eight hours after you take one, believe me, so Yather will be in charge during that period. He keeps your sidearm. Unloaded and secured. We monitor you for a couple of weeks. We keep working. No one's the wiser."

"That sounds ideal," Tzajos said heartily, buttoning up his shirt. "Superb. An excellent example of problem-solving. Do you have everything you need for the medication? Is there anything we need to purchase here? I notice the villagers aren't very consistent about giving receipts, and—"

"And there's no other symptoms?" Rothkard said, casting his eyes at the floor again. "Nothing you're not telling me?"

I am filled with the voices of the dead, I am filled with their words. They are crowding out my own. I see their memories, their last moments. Nothing that made it into the pitiful notebooks buried in the thick wet clay. I am the hated vessel of their last words. They are alive in me and

I don't know what they want or what they will do. "No! Nothing. Just these...funny spells."

"And you didn't have these before deployment? Only now?"

"Well, I wasn't overworked before this mission, was I?" Tzajos snapped. "Don't be ridiculous. How would I have passed the draft board if this was happening all the time?"

"I don't know," Rothkard said. "But it's possible. All sorts of things slip through because the draft doctor only looks at someone for ten minutes."

"You're suggesting that *I*—"

"No! No, sir."

"Good." He stabbed the last button through the last hole, jerked his belt straight, threw the strap of his satchel over his head, and glared at Rothkard and Yather. "Right. Supplies. Let's go."

The village had no official medical facility, which did not surprise Tzajos; like most places, it relied on the cobbling together of knowledge from several laymen, so that, like an illustrated plate in a book, eventually the single colors would combine to create a coherent picture. Usually between butchers and midwives you would have sufficient expertise to deal with a broken collarbone, a stuck baby, a poisonous mushroom, a wolf attack, or the sundry other disasters that tended to befall rural communities, but little more advanced than that.

Still, with the market in town, the elders had set up a big canvas stall specifically to deal with the population influx that might need a veterinarian or healer, marked with fluttering white ribbons probably meant to represent bandages. Tzajos went in first, scanning the place for someone with authority—there had to be someone, surely, triaging people as they came in and assigning them to a bed. Because there were beds, a dozen cots along each side of the stall, and a wide middle aisle lined with tables, crates, bags, wooden spindles of pre-torn bandages, and a small fire under a huge brass pot of water. It was crowded but relatively quiet, hardly the chaos that Tzajos experienced in city clinics or hospitals back home; the atmosphere was one of chummy resignation, an almost collegial "Oh well, now we've done it" expression on the patients lying or sitting in the beds.

Several people turned to stare at their uniforms, but no one confronted them. Tzajos sighed. "Hello there!" he said loudly. "Who's in charge, please?"

An elderly woman approached from the back of the room, silver hair pulled back into a tight bun, hands clean but light-blue sleeves bloodied to the elbow; what a *curious* set of colorings you saw here, Tzajos marveled. Such dark red-brown skin, and yet such green eyes. Like Lieutenant Calamuk, whose eyes you did not even realize were blue until you got right close. And the children—brown skin and blonde hair, olive skin and eyes the kind of brown that was almost red, white eyebrows and brown hair. Nothing like Treotan. "You," he said in his best Dastian. It seemed easier these days for some reason. "You're in command here?"

"I'm trying to make sure everyone sees a healer," she said tiredly. "If that's what you're asking. Do you need one?"

"No, no. We are looking to requisition... I mean, to get supplies," he corrected himself; he did not want to have to fill out an official requisition form afterward, and to falsify one would mean disaster in the next audit. Easier to sidestep it entirely. "We can pay."

She shrugged. "If you can find it, help yourselves. Leave us a little, that is all I ask." From her dress pocket she retrieved a complicated iron key on a leather braid, and unlocked a nondescript cabinet next to the cauldron of hot water.

"Thank you," Tzajos said. "I shall be sure to mention this village's cooperation to my superiors when I return."

But she was already gone, heading past them to the front of the tent, where a party of some half-dozen people had come in, calling for help.

"Do you see what you need?" Tzajos said to Rothkard, opening the portable apothecary cabinet and ignoring the prominent PROPERTY OF THE TREOTAN GOVERNMENT stamp on the inside of the door. The labels had all been scraped off the drawers, jars, and bottles; goodness only knew what was in them now. Most of them looked as if they had been refilled with herbs, and he was about to joke about this to Rothkard, perhaps a comment on their wives' spice cabinets at home, except was the man married? He could not remember.

He turned anyway, realizing that Rothkard was staring at the newcomers—dusty young men in the baggy trousers and close-fitting shirts and vests common around here, all insisting that their own injuries were mild—though Tzajos could see even from here the blood dripping on the grass inside the tent—and they must help instead their cousin, who had been burned.

"Hot oil," one of them seemed to be saying in a low, urgent voice to the silver-haired woman. "Do you understand? He is a seller of *knirinas*, the pot tipped over. The oil splashed him."

If she replied, Tzajos did not hear it; the woman turned away from him and began calling for helpers to carry the burned teenager to a clean cot, to get wax for ointments, clean bandages, other things he could not translate. "Rothkard!" he said again, stepping aside to let the litter pass. "Did you find what you need?"

"I—no. Let's go back out."

"What?"

"*Please*, sir," Yather said; Tzajos looked between them, baffled, but followed them back outside, ceding their spot to the woman and her assistants.

The market was still in full swing, the air filled with cries for fruit and vegetables, pickles, spreads, preserved meats, livestock, services—"Step up and write down the name of your farm for my prize boar! Stud guaranteed in two visits or less! Prize winning!"—breads, cheeses, jewelry, clothing, furniture, leather. Tzajos followed behind the other two, his confusion only growing, till Rothkard gestured them behind a stall selling some kind of omelet-in-a-bun, whose uninterrupted clatter of metal spatulas against metal griddle covered their conversation.

"Those weren't oil burns," Rothkard said. Yather nodded vigorously.

"So?" Tzajos said.

"I...you didn't smell it, did you?" Rothkard said. He looked up at Yather.

"I did," Yather said. "Sir, that lad bombed himself. I'd stake a month's pay on it."

"What?" But Tzajos was already returning to the moment in his mind's eye, picking apart everything he'd missed and furious that the other two had caught it instead of him: six young *men*, in a region where they were virtually all below the ground (or, now, in the back of one of the steam-tracks). Six young men all injured to some degree, as if they had been caught by the edge of a blast—not of hot oil or a grease fire, but an explosive that had gone wrong. And he had caught the acrid smell of sulfur, because he was too late to hold his breath as the litter had passed him, trying to avoid inhaling the odor of the boy's burnt flesh.

"Did they see us?" he said.

"Hard to imagine they didn't," Yather said. "But if they did, I hope it were just a quick peek. Good thing Rothers here got us out, eh?"

"But I didn't get what I needed for your sleeping pills, sir," Rothkard said.

Tzajos turned on his heel, paced a few steps, turned again. The stall-owner had his back to them, a big old man who seemed to have eight arms all flying between egg, bun, griddle, onions, oil-bottle; he paid them not the slightest bit of attention. But he would remember seeing them there later, if he was asked; Tzajos was sure of it. What did it mean? What did it mean? Nothing, perhaps. But a bomb. No, not a bomb: just a gruesomely injured young man, and the smell of a bomb.

And a lie to someone who could not possibly care whether they were lying or not. "What's *knirinas*?"

"A kind of dumpling," Yather said. "They make balls of dough and drop them into hot oil, and when they come out they put spices on them."

Tzajos chewed on his lip, which hurt more than he was expecting. He wondered if he had bitten it earlier when his men jumped on him in the post office. What a long day it had been, what a blessing that every minute that passed was a minute he would not have to re-experience. His stomach was churning. No proof of anything, no proof.

"A group of young men, dressed in local clothes," he said slowly. "New clothes they bought here to blend in, not the ones they brought from...wherever they're from. A group of young men in a country without young men. Who have found each other and perhaps made common cause against...something, some injustice that they hate. Experimenting with ways to defeat this... injustice. Learning how to be fighters. Not soldiers. There is no one they wish to take orders from. But fighters. And the villages they pass through, when they need food or medical supplies...everyone keeps the secret. Sometimes because they don't think there are insurgents in their midst. Some because they are complicit. Or even pleased. Because what could be more of a miracle now than seeing a young man alive?"

Rothkard said nothing. Yather said, "They must've come in from quite a way."

"They'll be recruiting," Tzajos said. "They don't want to build an army as big as the one we fought, and they can't anyway. But if they can get enough fighters, they think they can pick off the...the occupying forces before they've become properly entrenched. This wouldn't be fighting like the war. This would be something else."

"Sir," Yather said doubtfully, and it was amazing, wasn't it, how much emotion he was always able to put into a single word. A real talent.

Tzajos stared up at the nearer of the enormous black monoliths enclosing the village, at the infinite facets on it, some as small as the face on a playing card, some as big as a farmer's field. From a distance it looked perfectly smooth. Like a droplet of pitch. "Something else," he repeated. "They learned their lesson—what happens when you engage the Treotan army in a fair fight. So they would have resolved to stop fighting fair. Now they will dig in, have to be lured out. Ambush, kill quickly, disappear again. Blend into the landscape even when it seems there is nowhere to hide. Fight at night. Sabotage vehicles. Poison wells. I don't know. It will be a long, ugly war of attrition."

"The war's over, sir."

"Thank you, Yather. I had not forgotten that." He turned on his heel again, feeling strangely light-headed, almost drunk. Deep inside he sensed the pressure of the clamoring voices that had plagued him for days—as if they had all agreed to push at the same time and in the same place. Like shoving a stuck vehicle out of mud. *One, two, three, heave!*

"What are we going to do?" Yather said. "This place doesn't have a cabling station either; we asked about it this morning when we were looking for the post office. We could send a letter back to HQ, I s'pose, but it would be...weeks, I don't know."

"Letters aren't considered secure anyway," Tzajos said. "No, before we send anything, we need more information."

Rothkard looked over his shoulder. "I think we're about to get some."

"Mm?"

———

It was a nice dungeon, Tzajos thought, barely deserving of the term. It was warm, first of all. And generally spotless, if you discounted the animals in various attitudes of repose around the room: three dogs, four cats, and an intricate wickerwork cage containing a somnolent pair of ruffled black doves. Tzajos was very much of the opinion that animals and humans should never share living space, because animals were inherently carriers of filth and disease. He decided not to share that opinion at this time, for several reasons, not least of which were the shackles and torture implements still prominently displayed on the walls.

"You should drink your tea," his host said. "You don't look good."

Yather picked up his cup at once, small as a thimble in his grip; Rothkard did not move, presumably because he did not wish to disturb the striped cat that had somehow fallen asleep in the cramped, to Tzajos' eye, space between his left hip and the side of the bench on which the two men sat.

Tzajos had his own chair, an uncomfortable wooden one, and his own small table and tea. He took the mug and held it in both hands, hoping they would stop shaking. "Thank you," he said, for perhaps the dozenth time since he had arrived.

There had been no violence, much to his combined relief and unease. He had thought they had every reason to be violent—to simply turn on the Treotan soldiers in their midst and erase them from the land. Especially after what had happened in the morning. But no, ten villagers armed with unidentifiable, freshly sharpened farm implements had simply approached the three men, asked for the commanding officer, and then told them they must come have a talk with the village elder.

The said elder was probably in her sixties, a squat crabapple of a woman who nevertheless gave the impression that she might leap up and expertly employ any of the torture implements in the room if the spirit moved her. While her voice was polite, her face was ever at odds: scowling so furiously that Tzajos felt threatened. The men with the farm tools had surrounded the building in a silent and menacing cordon, guarding the doors and windows.

"This building used to belong to Kotor Morequa. You know who that was?" she said abruptly.

"Yes, elder," Tzajos said. "We were, er, here earlier today. In a different wing of the house. The dairy."

"We rose up together and killed him," she said, and Tzajos knew that she meant both *we* as in the Dastians of the region and a *we* that included her, personally, even though this had happened two hundred years ago, because history moved differently for these people. He couldn't remember how he knew it, only that he was right.

"Yes, elder," he said, since she seemed to expect some kind of response.

Her face darkened. "You know why?"

Tzajos raised his cup and drank; something was circling inside him, not like water, not flowing. Something with bones. Moving through grass. He thought of the old man's white dog, how for just a moment it seemed he could hear its thoughts. He thought of how the voices inside him—*Shut up! Leave me alone! Get out of me!*—knew the answer to the old woman's question. He thought of how he could not possibly know what the Kotor had looked like when he was alive, because there were no images of him in here, but he still did; he knew the face, he could have drawn it as if from life. The line of the nose, the curve of the upper lip, the emerald earrings on both ears.

The tea was bitter, very strong. It fell into his empty stomach like a dropped stone; he felt the invisible inhabitants sip greedily at it, a taste of home.

She said, "Because he was a *ryrroskos*...you don't know that word. Your army did not teach you that word. See it in your face. He did what you are doing. Do you understand that? He was digging up the dead and doing...*things* to them. *Rskalanarn*, magic. Not exactly magic. You don't know the other word either," she added exasperatedly.

I do, I do now. There is knowledge inside me. I did not ask for this. They know all the words you are using. They swim inside me thick as eels in a tank, slithering, snapping, biting. They want to crawl out and escape. They can breathe both water and air. Tzajos realized he was trembling again, and put his tea cup back on the table. "We are here on a mission of mercy," he recited mechanically, "a charitable—"

"Shut up. They told me what happened this morning, what you did with your gun."

"I... No one was hurt, I didn't—"

"You think we don't know anything out here," she said. "That is what you think, all of you. You think: Why did we bother taking over this country of cave-men? They are ignorant, they are backwards, children. So you tell yourself, I wouldn't ask permission before I did something to my child. You came here, without asking, without receiving consent, and you..."

"We did the same for our own soldiers!" Tzajos blurted. "It's—wouldn't you want the same? Why wouldn't you want that? Our families back home in Treotan, they all wanted to know what had happened to their sons, brothers, fathers, husbands. Don't you want to be able to go to these people and say, yes, we know what happened? Here are the remains?"

The elder stared at him, aghast. "Monsters," she said softly. "*Monsters*. No. The dead must be buried where they fall. As close as can be managed. So the spirit can rest. Everything complete, together. And never touched again. Never, ever, ever. What did you believe would happen when you violated and stole our dead? Nothing? Is that what *your* people believe? Well, you are wrong. And now you are suffering the consequences."

There it was. Out in the open where no one could deny it—where three separate Treotan soldiers, Tzajos thought numbly, would have to deny it if they were court-martialed. The fire crackled and popped. What time was it? He felt he could not lift his wrist to check; it felt too heavy, or out of his control. "What's happening to me?" he managed hoarsely. "Calamuk knew something..."

"Who?"

"Our interpreter. A Dastian man. He knew... He did not tell me..."

"You have been eating of the dead," she said, leaning forward in her chair. Her eyes were red, verging on maroon; they burned under her white lashes. "You took their bones, you took their words. You read things you were never meant to read. Those words are for the dead. Not the living. You ate their spirit—"

"No!"

"*Yes*. I don't know how. But it's like Kotor Morequa, it's the same sickness. It's in you, it comes off you—a smell, a reek of the dead. You read too many of their words and you let them *into yourself*, you broke their sleep, they are crazed without rest, they are not meant to be awake again, alive again—"

"They're not!" Tzajos cried, staggering to his feet so abruptly he knocked over his chair as well as the table beside it. The mug broke on the stone floor, splashing him with cold tea. "They're not! That's insane! *I've been shot and I don't even know it's the shot that killed me because it hurts of course it hurts a little bit but not much blood and I can still shoot I can still fight I can still—*"

The words flooded from him hot as vomit; the room went dim. Clarity returned seconds later as the elder picked him off the floor, pinning him to the wall with one hand at his throat. She was not squeezing, but the pressure was enough to let him know that if she wanted to, it would be over in a second—before Yather or Rothkard could do anything. They were frozen anyway, staring at him from the bench. Near the wall, a dog looked up sleepily, then put its head down again. No danger.

"What's going to happen to me?" Tzajos managed. "Please, tell me... Can someone get them out of me? Can this be cured? I can't go back like this, I can't. They'll lock me up, they'll..."

She watched him babble without sympathy till he ran down, then released her grip on his throat and stepped back, straightening her elder jacket, black velvet and silver thread. "Sometimes a sickness cannot be cured," she said flatly. "Sometimes, we see a mad dog, and we have to stop it from biting others because the dog itself cannot..."

Tzajos stared at her, horrified.

"Get one of them to do it," she said, gesturing at Yather and Rothkard. "It's a gun. It will be very quick. Or you can do it yourself—but I don't think you will be able to. It's not in you."

You don't know me, he wanted to say, but he found he could say nothing; he had no words of his own.

"Then it will be the other thing, if you can't or won't," she said. "Your men will kill you. Rip you apart, maybe. Or we will."

"Can't I...can't I control it, can't I learn how to live w—"

"You've already shown that you can't," she said.

"What do they want from me?" he wailed, slumping to the floor.

"What do you *think* they want from their violator?" she said, turning away from him. "*Revenge*." She pointed at Yather. "You, big man. You have two guns. Give me that one, the little one. I'll finish this right now."

Yather began to reach for one of his pistols, perhaps some atavistic or childish part of him responding to the authority in the woman's voice rather than the words themselves, then hesitated, looking down at Tzajos. "Er, sir," he began.

Tzajos opened his mouth but, realizing he had no idea who or what might respond, quickly closed it again and put both his hands over it. *Don't kill me, please, Yather*, he wanted to shout, but what if one of the dead men said something else? What if *they* begged Yather to kill his commander, in his voice?

He could not even remember Yather's first name to appeal to him. He was useless, a stranger to his men, a liability. He squeezed his eyes shut. The spilled tea was soaking into his trousers, making him wonder, for a second, whether he had wet himself. He opened his eyes again. Maybe it *would* be better to die, rather than live like this—as someone not himself. As dozens of someones.

"All right," he said rapidly, getting up, scraping his hands on the stone wall, speaking in Treotan in his rush. "All right, all right, listen, all of you listen to me—"

"Sir, they can't understand you," Rothkard said.

Tzajos wasn't listening. "What if I—simply apologized to them? Yes, what if I did that? If I said I was sorry, if I said I understood I had offended them, you know, I didn't respect their *custom*, if I said *no but you will never say sorry for the war never you said came here to kill us kill us kill all of us you said teach them some respect for their new masters you said we were dogs you said we were cattle you said children savages barbarians said we were wasting what we had and you would take it for the common good*—"

He ran out of air and gasped for breath, releasing it again in a shuddering wail that resembled the cry of the violet foxes, *Play with us! Come play!* but no one was looking at him any more—the elder, Yather, and Rothkard were staring at the windows, where the guards had begun to shout warnings to one another. The clash of metal against metal sang into the room like bells.

This was it! His men had come to save them! The unit had noticed they were missing, discovered their location, and ridden to the rescue! Tzajos felt a minute of genuine hope, fading swiftly as he realized he had heard no gunshots. The noises of the fight were primeval: scythes, hoes, clubs, knives.

As the unlocked door swung open, two of the dogs in the dungeon stood, their tails wagging uncertainly, giving no indication they meant to attack. Perhaps they did not smell something unfamiliar, Tzajos thought; or perhaps they simply needed to be ordered to do so. Military dogs then, soldier dogs. Good: someone here had some discipline. The village elder crossed her arms, careful to ensure that her necklace bearing the heavy lead amulet embossed with the town seal remained visible, and faced the newcomers.

Three young men, almost boys—their faces still soft with baby fat, jarringly at odds with their set, grim expressions. These were the eyes of boys who had killed, who had broken something inside themselves like a bone to allow themselves to kill. They were no longer thinking of their father's farm, raising animals, courting girls. They had had another future presented to them and had left all that behind, hoping perhaps that the next generation, if there was one, could take it over.

The leader, who had curling unruly brown hair shot through with gold, pointed at them with his sword— unbloodied, Tzajos noticed, but that did not mean anything. Perhaps he had wiped it outside. He said, "Elder, is that him? By the fire? The *ryrroskos*?"

She glared at him, uncowed. "Who are you?"

His gaze flicked down to the amulet, back up to her face. Would he disobey the elder? Their word was supposed to be absolute. The boy said, "We are the ones who have come here to get this man. Is it him?"

"You have come to kill him?"

"We have come because our leader said to take him away," the boy said. "We have all the others."

The others? His men? All of them? No, it was a lie, it must be a lie. They had emphasized that again and again in the briefings: They're not *like* us. They don't think of the *truth* the same way we do. It's cultural. Like their religions, like their vendettas, like the way they name their villages and children—they think everything is a story. They are always telling a story.

Maybe he meant...maybe he means they have *spoken* to the men. Convinced them Tzajos was ill, needed help. *We'll take care of it for you, we'll cure him.* So "have" meant only "have captured their consent." Something like that.

The elder said, "I am telling you to kill him."

"We are not going to kill him."

"I am *telling you.*"

"No."

A blur, and another blur. Tzajos and all his cursed inhabitants watched, stunned, as the elder lunged for Yather's gun, as the boy with the curly hair put his body between them, as Yather himself got his hands up to fight, as the dogs soared up like thrown spears. It was over in an instant.

The fighters may have been young, but they had been training hard, or someone had been training them; they disarmed and bound Yather and Rothkard in moments, then stepped over the prone bodies of the cursing village elder and her softly whimpering dogs.

Tzajos thought about putting his fists up, getting in one good swing, at least while Yather was watching him before he was dragged outside. Instead he watched dazedly as they tugged him to the door, knotted rope at his wrists and ankles—good knots, much better than he knew how to do, probably some agricultural thing—and threw him onto a waiting cart.

––––––––––––

In Tzajos's nightmares, if he had imagined such a thing happening to him, the kidnappers put a hood over his head or bound his eyes so he could not see where they were taking him, presumably so he would be too afraid to go far even if he managed to escape. Instead, they rolled out of the village in broad daylight, the horses not even trotting but walking, and everyone in the market—*everyone*—studiously ignoring the bound men on the floor of the wooden cart. Turning their heads away with a slow deliberate movement, not looking up at the boys who had kidnapped them either. We saw nothing, we saw nothing. We did not see their faces, no. We know they were not local. No, they came here, and then they left. We did not see which way they went.

He tried to remember his anti-interrogation training—it had been so long ago, in his early training, and so vague, so unhelpful, it had assumed you would be captured during combat, that there would be whole units assigned to rescue you before you talked. And what would he have been able to reveal anyway? He knew nothing of strategy, troop movements, attacks, timing. He worked in an accounting and supply office, far from the front. He had never killed, never watched anyone die. He had used his sidearm only at the training range. At some point, everyone counselled him, he *would* be called up—they would all leave the office, get onto a train, and head out there to this mysterious place called East Seudast to fight. But it never happened. And then the war was over. It seemed very unfair that he should be captured and tortured now.

His whole body oozed sweat despite the cold breeze; he was sure he stank of fear, that the others could smell it. *Yellow-belly, lily-liver!* the other men would have whispered. Yather said nothing; Rothkard had curled into a ball as best he could with his arms bound behind him and seemed to be sleeping. They did not speak to him, the fighters also did not speak to him, they furthermore did not speak to each other. When the driver clucked to the horses it seemed as loud as a shout.

Tzajos wriggled around, attracting no attention, till he could sit up and press his back to the side of the cart, letting him look around. Another *bloody* lizard in here. He ignored it. In the distance through the mist he saw the muddy brown line of where their steam-tracks had traveled, and tried to get his bearings. They were headed roughly north and east, he thought. A region still covered by his precious sector map, where there were many grids to complete, though these were supposed to be done last, according to his plan.

All around there was nothing but sky, fog, green grass, birds, the irregular black stones. Some were no higher than a door-stop, some bigger than a mountain. They followed no rhyme or reason to his eye, but he knew that the local people used them as landmarks, could calculate precise times and distances between each, were never lost so long as they knew the closest stone. It was like telling someone back home the street and avenue at which they might seek out the address they had been given.

"I'm sorry, chaps," Tzajos said hours later, as the sun began to sink. His throat stung from dehydration; his voice sounded rusty and false. "This is my fault."

Yather shook his head in silence; Rothkard managed to murmur, "It isn't. You're sick, that's all. It's a disease. All their talk of...spirits, ghosts. I couldn't follow it all. But it can't be true."

"That moment with the Recovery Unit," Tzajos said. "Something happened. I think it... They've always believed something like this was *possible*. That if you disturb the dead even to recover them, treat them with care and respect, return them to their families...it stirs something up. It gives them a path. That's why you don't do it. And *certainly* never to read their words. That was how they came out, at first...into my letters. Into my notebook."

Rothkard sighed. "So you lied to me when I asked. Right to my face you lied. Sir."

"I...I'm sorry for that too. I thought it was just...like you said. Stress, overwork." He watched the other man's mop of dark hair droop lower, lower, till chin touched chest.

"It's all right," Yather said quietly. "You weren't to know, neither of you. I mean," he attempted a chuckle, "who'd have believed it even if we was told in advance? Not me."

Tzajos watched the sun sink, slow, staining the mist. Like blood seeping into a linen bandage—no. He pushed the image away. That last skull they had found, perfectly clean and white as a porcelain bowl for some reason, the long legbones not fused yet: the body of a teenager, thirteen or fourteen maybe. Washed clean in the Mule's water spray like all the others but shining even brighter than that. As if it was not bone but stone. A precious gem.

The stronghold of the insurgents—or these ones, anyway—was, as Tzajos had suspected and feared, inside one of the great black monoliths. Wordless, they were trussed and hauled on ropes like sacks of wheat, up, up, sickeningly high, easily more than a hundred yards up the side of the stone. The darkness was its own blessing, since Tzajos could not then see the entire landscape spread out below them. He had known he disliked heights but not to this extent; or perhaps he had never been so high in his life. In Treotan, in his home city, he had been in a twelve-story building once, the pride of its builders. But this, this would be...his mind balked at the calculation. Thirty stories? Thirty-five?

Inside the stone, after a winding tunnel, a surprisingly capacious room had been chipped out, all gleaming black walls lit with small glass lanterns. No open flames here, sensibly. Couldn't escape a blaze from this height. Like a fire at sea. The rounded walls were lined with fighters and supplies, leaving a large open area in the center, which contained something like a watchtower—a hip-high block of stone big enough for four men to sit comfortably, each watching a quadrant of the room and holding one of the decades-old shotguns that Seudast had used in the war.

Contraband! Tzajos almost exclaimed, then laughed at himself. What did these secret fighters care for the terms of the armistice? The important thing, at any rate, was that his unit was there—in the dim light he could not quite make out faces, but he could see uniforms, and he could count. Only one missing. Yather would know who.

As his eyes adjusted he realized, too, that some of the fighters were women—many quite young themselves, in their late teens or early twenties, dressed like the others in wide trousers tucked into thick-soled leather boots, long-sleeved flax shirts under long vests, like a uniform. The ones with long hair had tied it up in plaits or buns, unlike the men, who let theirs flow and tangle on their shoulders. Tzajos did not doubt that the women would be as willing to torture, fight, and kill as the men. Women were not allowed in the Treotan armed forces, except in very personnel-strapped areas as administrative support, kept far from the front (like him, but he did not like to think about that). No Dastian women's names were listed on his official catalog of the dead to recover. But it seemed that now, they had signed up to fight—filling the gap left by a war that had killed nearly all the young men.

"You!" shouted someone in Treotan, a dry-throated roar. "You little bastard! This is all your fault! We wasn't supposed to be in combat!"

Tzajos flinched; his captor shoved him ahead, boots slipping on the glassy floor. "I know—" he began, unheard.

"You son of a bitch!" the man screamed. "You never knew what you were doing out here! We should throw you out this thing!"

"Shut up!" someone shouted back. "It doesn't matter whose fault it is!"

"Be a man, stop whining like a dog!"

"Suck it up and hold it in!"

"It's his doing! That posh little fuck with the mustache! Take him and let the rest of us go!"

"Shut up or I'll shut you up, you shit-bottomed brat!"

A few of the Dastians went along the line of seated men, dispensing kicks and slaps to quiet the captured soldiers; if they had understood the content of the argument, they gave no indication. Tzajos was struck again, this time with a cold thrill of fear, at how quiet they were—they had not spoken on the cart ride here, but inside their hideout they were not joking or chatting with one another either, as he was used to seeing from his men. Their silence bothered him, or the restraint bothered him—it did not seem natural for young people to act like this. Like automatons created for war. As advanced as Treotan weaponry was, they had created no such thing; yet Seudast had succeeded, and here they were.

Someone wrestled Tzajos easily to a bare spot on the floor, pushing him to sit. Then the fighter stepped back, and another took his place, this one carrying a small lantern—no, not one of the insurgents. Lieutenant Calamuk, still in his uniform trousers, his regulation shirt and jacket replaced with a long-sleeved white shirt and a black wool cloak covered in tiny blue embroidery, too intricate to see. His face was not hard and emotionless like the others; he seemed resigned, even saddened, as he stooped next to Tzajos.

"They wanted to break your legs to make sure you would stay where you were put," he said in Treotan. "I asked them not to. So please do not do anything dangerous. Do what they tell you to do."

"I...I will."

"Good." Calamuk sighed, rubbing his eyes, the blue circles under them deepened now into black, like day-old bruises. "You're angry, hm? You think, *Of course the interpreter betrayed us. He's been doing it since the start.* No, I didn't. I have been with them only hours—only since this morning. When I saw what happened at the post office."

"It doesn't matter when," Tzajos said. "You did still betray us. You signed an oath to the Treotan army, and now you have broken it to...to do what? You can't fight us, you...you handful of children. Look at them, Calamuk! Why did you do it?"

"It doesn't make sense to you?" Calamuk said. "For you, the Treotan empire—yes, even though you have no emperor—is like a strong house. It keeps you safe. Thick walls. For me it was like a prison. Those also have thick walls. After the war, I thought if I signed up, I could send money home, keep my surviving family safe—my cousins, my grandparents, aunts, uncles. My parents died in the war. My brothers and sister died too. I thought the killing was over. But I began to hear about those re-education camps Treotan has set up in the interior. About the farms they promised such a good life on—about the mines, the forests, the places Treotan is moving my people. Not to have a good life. To be slaves, or less than slaves, because they are also defeated. Just labor."

Tzajos stared at him, genuinely stunned. "No. No! That's not happening. We wouldn't...it's just...settling... it's settling the unsettled areas. To help Seudast get back on its feet after the war—be a productive part of Treotan. It's to *help*. Like our mission!"

"People are dying," Calamuk replied, shaking his head. "No, people are being *killed*. It's been going on since the first camp. The Treotan administration is murdering people. But they don't see it that way, because murder is for human beings, and my people aren't people. They're..." He stared up at the glittering roof, studying their many tiny reflections, as if searching out the correct word. "Productive hours."

"Calamuk..."

"I have no one left for them to threaten now," he said. "No one left to kill. Thanks to Treotan. I thought it couldn't be true. But too many people have told me the same thing—too many people have seen it, fled it, tried to warn others."

"So that's why you took us?" Tzajos said. "Revenge? You want everyone to know that, what, your people refute the non-aggression pact we signed at the end of the war, that you still want a fight?"

"No, we don't want a fight." He sighed again. "I am so tired, Tzajos. I didn't want any of this. You know, it's funny that the young soldiers called you cockroaches? It's not strictly about hostility—about hating a roach, about personally wanting it to die at your hand. It's also because roaches are low to the ground. They barely see a world bigger than themselves. That's like you, like all of Treotan, not just the soldiers."

"That's completely untrue," Tzajos said, offended. "We're exceedingly cosmopolitan. We see the entire world, we see more of the world than anyone."

"No you don't. You only see what you put your name on—that's all that's real to you, that's all that has meaning. Everything else is mists and shadows, it's not unexplored or unfamiliar to you, it's simply...unclaimed. That's the *only* word you have to describe everything that's not yours. Nothing else. Not until you own it do you care."

Calamuk put his hands on his thighs and rose slowly, handing the lantern off to one of the fighters—the expressionless boy with the curly, brindle-striped hair who had hit the village elder.

"What happens now?" Tzajos said, hating the whine in his voice, hating that the men could hear it.

"We are waiting for someone to come to us," Calamuk said, turning away; the cloak made him all but invisible from the back. "Then we will have a talk about why you are here, and why you are alive for now."

Tzajos was not sure how much time passed after that conversation; the voices within him were quiet, seething, but seemed content to watch rather than act up for the time being. He and his soldiers were fed twice, he was not sure how many hours apart—a slice of thick black bread and a rock-hard lump of salty sheep's cheese the first time, only bread the second. They were given water from a communal wooden bucket that one of the younger fighters walked with down the line of captives, allowing a sip or two per man. The Dastians drank tea and ate the army rations seized from the captured convoy, heated up on the portable stove and eaten from stolen mess kits, further incensing Tzajos.

He did nothing. He could do nothing. He kept imagining the sounds his legs would make as they broke them; he tried to stop and could not. It turned his stomach in a neverending revolution, like the rubber-and-steel treads of a steam-track. He had never heard a bone break. Not for the first time he thought perhaps he had lived too sheltered a life. It was a pity that would never change now.

Sheer exhaustion let him sleep a few times, despite his bonds and the noise, the hard floor, the cold wind blowing constantly through the entrance tunnel. Sleep was a relief; he wished he could spend all his time there. If only Rothkard could have gotten those pills made up! He could have, perhaps, surreptitiously taken them all now—slept forever—escaped whatever was coming next, which could not be good, and he feared it all the more for Calamuk's vagueness about it. But no—he did not think he could kill himself. Even now, in this hopeless place. It wasn't that he thought he could out-think them, out-negotiate them, escape even. Only that he had nothing but his life, as shameful and small as it was, and he could not give up the only thing he had.

The newcomer came several hours after the second piece of bread, announced by the grating rasp of the ropes in the pulley, dragging Tzajos out of another uneasy half-sleep. A boot thumped into his ribs, not hard.

The curly-haired boy. Holding a sword easily at his side—no, something cruder, a machete, sharp and chipped. "Get up," the boy said.

Was this it? His death? Were they waiting only for the visitor to witness his execution? Or complete it? Tzajos rose clumsily, and now all he could think of was the boy's heavy machete-blade going through the back of his neck. *Crunch!* Would one blow be enough? He hoped so. Maybe it would not even hurt too badly. Considerate of them, actually, to allow him such a swift death. Unless they wanted to torture him first. Perhaps that's who they had invited—a torturer!

The visitor was a middle-aged woman, tall, almost as tall as Yather, swathed in an elaborate shawl embroidered in blues and greens over a long black dress. Her black hair was scraped back severely from her high, noble forehead and long, thin nose. Eyes dark blue, like Calamuk's, but flecked with paler specks—like a dusk sky full of stars.

"This is it?" she said in Dastian, a regional accent Tzajos did not recognize. "The abomination? Him, this little one?"

"Yes," said the boy with the machete, stepping aside to let Calamuk through.

The woman snorted. "Can he understand us?"

"His Dastian has been improving greatly of late," Calamuk said.

Tzajos looked between them, panicked. The woman carried no weapons in her hands, which were powerful, adorned with a half-dozen rings each—gems, brass, silver, wood. But she also had a big leather satchel. Maybe the torture instruments were in there? "How do you do, madam," he croaked in his best Dastian. "Major Lyell Tzajos, at your service."

She did not smile. "At my service, Tzajos? Good. My name is Alyea. The others here have false names, war names. Not me. I am not fighting. I am here to do a job. You should make it easy for me. You understood all that?"

Tzajos nodded, mouth dry. Training. Interrogation. Something. Supposed to resist until you were rescued, or provoke until they killed you (which they might do accidentally anyway, as the torture escalated). Say nothing. No betrayal. Enough traitors here. Stay strong. What was in the satchel? No, don't look at it. One thing they suggested was to name all the animals starting with a certain letter, to occupy the mind, keep it off the pain. Pick a letter at random. G...Grasshopper. Giraffe. Grass-snake. G...g...

A thick, waiting hush, as of a theater before the curtains went up. For no reason he thought of the capital back home, where it was said the highest officers and government officials had a ceremony they did in a theater with prisoners of war. Like him, like now. But the Dastians wouldn't know about that. They wanted something from him and on principle, whatever it was, he must not let them have it.

Goldfinch. Gecko.

Grave-beetle.

She opened the satchel and withdrew not the screws and blades of a torturer, but a sheaf of paper, quite ordinary paper, like any school loose-leaf you would buy in a shop. Plain white paper with blue lines. At her gesture, two of the fighters brought empty wooden crates—one for her to sit on, one for Tzajos (he obeyed her every gesture), and one between them, on which she placed the paper and a lantern.

"What has happened to you should not have been allowed to happen," she said quietly. From the corner of his eye, Tzajos could see the others straining to listen, leaning forward but not daring to move. Who was this woman, what hold did she have over them, Treotan and Dastian alike?

"The elder in Khuverban would have killed you simply for being what you are," Alyea said. "For no other reason. Later, it would be considered a mercy—your men would say, *Thank the gods he did not continue to suffer.* But the villagers did not wish to bestow mercy on you. And you deserve none anyway. We took you away not to kill you—yet—but because you are a weapon."

"I...what? No, I'm not. I'm..."

"You already know you are. You are filled not only with knowledge of your own forces, but ours—and you know where fighting happened, where men died, what they left behind, everything at the moment of death that we have no other ways of knowing. Because you are filled with the spirits of the dead men. They are in you. They can answer questions you do not even know the answers to, they can dig into you and find out. You stole them, and you tried to put them into little glass boxes— but you couldn't control them."

Oh, it's not glass, actually, Tzajos almost said. *It's a type of synthetic material, and—* He shook his head sharply. "You are asking me for military intelligence?" he said formally. "I can't. I am under orders to die first."

Alyea looked at him for a long time, and Tzajos felt something approaching a swell of pride, cutting through his terror and shame—pride that he had stood up to her, that he had done something his men could respect. The code of silence: they all knew about that. None of them would have talked, in his position. They would have all said the same thing as him.

No signal seemed to pass between them, but the curly-haired boy went to the wall, returned dragging one of Tzajos's men—Vzeath, the youngster who had helped pull him from the stream. The boy's face was stark white beneath its moonscape of freckles and spots, his gingery eyebrows standing out like two stripes of red ink. No one protested.

"Valens," Alyea said. "Just a little. Ear, finger, toe. All right?"

"Foot? It would be easier. Then I don't have to take off the boot," the curly-haired boy—Valens—said.

"No, that's too much. He'll die."

"You can survive losing one foot," Valens said, annoyed. "If it's a clean cut, it's no problem."

Vzeath stared up at them in what seemed like genuine disbelief. "What are they saying, sir?" he whispered.

"Leave the boy alone," Tzajos said, and switched languages with a grunt of effort. "It's all right. It's just a threat—they want me to inform on our military and they have taken," he added, raising his voice, "the coward's way out, by threatening one of my men instead of me."

Calamuk shook his head. "They are doing that because there are more of your men," he explained. "If they kill one—on purpose or by accident—then there is another. And the others will hate you more. Please cooperate with her, major. She will have the boy do whatever it takes. And he will not hesitate."

"Leave him alone! Why not put the blade to me instead?" Tzajos said, his voice trembling as Valens forced Vzeath to the floor, knelt on his back, and held the boy's arm out—his left, which was some small blessing anyway, Tzajos's mind bleated thoughtlessly, *unless the boy's a leftie, which I've never paid attention to, Yather would know, where's Yather? Why is he not at my side? Why don't they just rise up and kill them, kill these boys and girls, these peasants? Why will no one speak up?*

"Sir!" quavered Vzeath, his face pressed to the floor.

They will do it now. They will all rise up to save him. Maybe they would do it for me—maybe not. But they will rise up for him. Even if some of them die, the others will...will...*must...*

"Change your mind," Alyea said.

Tzajos shook his head mutely, seeking out the faces of his men against the wall. But it was too dark, and he could see only the ranks of their dark green jackets, lighter blurs above them.

Valens shrugged. The machete rose, glinting dully in the lantern-light.

"Lieutenant Calamuk!" said Tzajos. "Tell them to see reason! I order you to talk to them. This is not the way a civilized people—"

The blade descended, and there was a startled silence, longer than Tzajos would have thought credible, before Vzeath began to scream. Two fingers rolled a little way on the stone floor, then stopped, stuck in the pool of blood forming beneath the boy's hand. He rolled and bucked, trying to get out from under Valens, but could not escape, could only lie flat and scream into the floor.

"I'll do it!" Tzajos shouted. "I'll do it! Anything you want! Leave him alone, leave them all alone!"

Alyea smiled at last, showing sharp white teeth. "I am glad," she said. "There are ways to compel you to do it—so the old wisdom says. But it takes so long. This is easier for everyone. Don't you think?"

Tzajos barely heard her; he realized he was panting for breath, as if he had been running. Vzeath was dragged away again, into the darkness, presumably so they could bind his wound—or maybe not, who knew what these people would do—leaving only the blood shining on the floor, the red invisible against the black, so that it seemed as if motor oil had spilled, not blood at all. And the two fingers, inexplicably curled now, like quotation marks. Showing that something had been spoken.

———

Now time truly became a blur; he fell into a trance, only infrequently permitted to leave it to attend to the needs of his body, rushing in these brief lucid periods to obey the instructions of his captors, who would have preferred him to stay under and tell everything he knew. Everything the spirits knew too, he realized dimly. At first he could only watch and listen as they spoke, and could understand very little unless he looked down at the page where he was writing down their answers.

Their spoken Dastian—rapid, fluent, usually peppered with words in local dialects—was beyond him, and they did not always wish to speak through his mouth.

Here was where we

Give me the pencil, I will draw a map for you

The temple is here, see, and then to the northeast

My leg blood bleeding blood it won't stop it won't stop! It won't stop! I thought it was going to stop but it's still bleeding!

Don't listen to him

Their big vehicles were lined up just here, they cannot move farther

Yes, the marsh

Mama! Mama, where am I? They said I was hit, but

Shut up!

Some of the voices seemed well aware they were dead; others did not. Infrequently he recognized names of villages from his sector map, or dead soldiers to whom he had paid particular attention in the records, tracking an unusual spelling or distinguishing two similar names. His right hand cramped and flamed, and was sometimes immersed in a bucket of icy water; he howled at the pain, but it helped for a few hours afterward.

Why, why had they fought so hard? Why had the entire country mobilized at once—like a bar fight spilling into the street, every man operating as one, a single mind. Annexing should have been a bloodless business. It had been the case for other Treotan provinces. If East Seudast had simply agreed to the initial terms after that first skirmish at the border, then none of this would have happened. Just...just paperwork. And the lines on the map meant nothing, did they? Why fight so hard to defend it? And to lose, as they must have known they would.

Gunfire like stars in the darkness

Treotan had not *invaded*. They were hardly ancient barbarians galloping with bows and arrows and plague to the gates of some opulent fortified city. They had asked *nicely* and Seudast had said *Never, never, never, never*. And never was a long time. Much longer than a short war.

"They'll send someone for us," Tzajos said when he had a short break, some indefinable time later. Forty or fifty written pages lay on one side of the wooden crate; his mouth was so dry that his tongue was beginning to swell, his lips to crack. He licked greedily at the droplets of blood they produced, unable to stop himself.

Calamuk appeared silently, took a canteen out of his cloak; Tzajos hefted it in his palm for only a moment before putting it to his mouth. Less than a quarter full. Beggars, choosers. He emptied it quickly, feeling that he had swallowed nothing, that it had soaked into his tongue.

"Thank you," he said. He looked around, dazed. Alyea was gone, presumably asleep or otherwise occupied; the other fighters were sleeping or sitting on the ground in silence, watching the captured soldiers.

"They might send someone for you," Calamuk said. "You've told us the protocol."

"Have I."

"It would take them a long time to find us, I think." The interpreter took the canteen out of Tzajos's limp fingers. "A long, long time. Anything could happen between now and then."

"That lady, Alyea. Who is she? How did you get her to come here?"

"I suppose you would call her...a wizard? A sorcerer? A witch?" Calamuk rolled all the unfamiliar Treotan words in his mouth like olive stones. "She can talk to the spirits more easily than most. They trust her, they respect her. In their past lives they knew her or knew of her."

"Calamuk, you don't *really* believe that," Tzajos said, exhausted. "This is all..."

"Would you have believed anything that's happening to you?"

"I'd believe that I lost my mind from overwork and from reading too many journals written by dead men."

"But you won't believe *us* when we say that's not what's happening," Calamuk said.

"It's unscientific."

"So is life. You know, there was a time, Tzajos, when I thought to myself, *I could be friends with this man, maybe. Even though his people have killed my people and he treats me like a dog.* You know why? It was because when we met back at headquarters, before we shipped out, I heard you talk in one of your language classes— you brought up *Blikust tur Medusk, Darc tur Kotor Coskim. The Tale of the Basilisk and Kotor Coskim*, King Coskim, the king of the fairies. Officially that is not our national poem, but unofficially, everybody knows it."

"It was mentioned in the translation book given to officers," Tzajos said, closing his eyes. "So I looked it up." Everything hurt, from ankles to eyebrows, and the ache was only numbed a little with the cold. He wanted more water; he wanted the traitor to go away and leave him alone. But he also wanted him to stay—give him more of this human voice, so that he did not feel so hideously occupied and alone at the same time. Yather would have been better. But Yather was kept from him.

"You were the only Treotan who seemed to know about it," Calamuk said. He squatted next to Tzajos and tucked his arms into his cloak. "But even you didn't understand it. King Coskim was a real king, our king. Long, long ago. And the basilisk was real too, he and the creatures he commanded. Just another set of invaders in the long, long list who tramped through our home, demanding to be fed, worshipped, exalted, telling us to kill our fattest lambs—"

"And roast them over a bone-fire till all the land could smell it and everyone was so sick from the smell that they could not eat, and only the basilisk could eat," Tzajos recited slowly. "Yes. All right. An allegory, all right, fine."

"The basilisks are gone now," Calamuk said after a long pause. "They are part of Treotan. Even their language is gone. We had to take another word and give it to them so they had a name for the poem. Their own names are all gone. I thought you knew all that. Then I saw you didn't."

"Yes, yes, all right. *We're* the villains. *We* go around the world not even *offering* to ally with people and set up trade relationships, we just stomp in like playground bullies and take, take, take. Happy now?" Anger rose in him, weak but real, palpable as the faintest hint of warmth in his frozen innards. "None of that is true, and you know it! Why can't you people simply accept the *truth?* Seudast agreed to partner with us to develop their lead and silver mines, then *you* reneged on the deal, expelled us, and literally attacked our facility across the border in the dead of night afterwards. We simply acted to restore the original mining agreement and re-staff our joint mines, and Seudast overreacted like a petulant child, and that's how the conflict began. Everybody knows that. It was in the papers, for heaven's sake. *Worldwide.*"

"It was in the papers," Calamuk said. "Yes."

"Well, then." He hated the man's calm superiority, hated the apathy in the face of logic—the interpreter accepted none of this, he still believed it was untrue, he was only agreeing because he felt he was himself arguing with a child, and Tzajos hated that too.

"You see that man there?" Calamuk said quietly, pointing with his chin at Valens, dozing against the wall with the machete across his lap, nearly invisible in the gloom. "He joined with this cell a few months ago. He spoke no Dastian, no Treotan."

"Months? What? Where is he from?"

"He says he doesn't remember. I believe him, because Alyea believes him. She's good at spotting liars. But he also says..."

Tzajos was curious despite himself, despite the sickening memory of the blade coming down, the screams of his soldier ringing in his memory. "He says what."

"He says he has been in many revolutions before, and he will be in many in the future," Calamuk said, almost dreamily, as if reciting a sonnet. "He says he will always appear when he is needed to fight. In this lifetime, it is here. In past lifetimes, it was elsewhere."

"What?"

Calamuk shrugged. "Not everything can be explained with science. You don't know how that Recovery Unit works, do you?"

"Of course I do. It's *very* simple—it's scarcely different from the principle that transfers luminiferous ether to heat and light our homes in Treotan. The only difference between them is that ether arises from inanimate sources, and teleplasm is generated by animate ones. It's discharged as long as the animating principle is in effect, that is, while the being is alive; and when the principle ceases to be in effect, the accumulated teleplasm stays in the body until it naturally dissipates. Which means that, if not too much time has passed, we can collect it via suction and filtration using the Recovery Unit, which is tuned to its particular space in the etheric spectrum."

Calamuk nodded slowly. "So you would not say it is a soul."

"Two different words. It's no more a soul than the spark you see when you shuffle your stockinged feet across a wool rug."

"Then how *do* you explain the voices you hear inside you?"

Tzajos said nothing. Alyea was returning, her face set, already pointing silently at the unwritten pile of paper on the wooden crate.

"You," she said to Calamuk, "fetch a fresh lantern. And *you*. We have much to complete."

Days passed. Fighters came in and out, taking some of the soldiers as they went—spreading out the hostages, Tzajos realized dimly through his exhaustion. So that he would never really be sure who was dead, who was alive, and who was where. Weapons began to appear, or perhaps they did not and he was imagining them—he smelled gunpowder and the makings of gunpowder, the sour odor of agriculturally-derived explosives, fresh and old blood, fresh and old metal. Maps appeared too, pasted to the walls. A kittenish girl of thirteen or fourteen arrived and taught a class on silent methods of killing: knives, garrotes, specific damage to the spine and the throat.

It would still not be war, Tzajos thought. Not war, something else. Just...fighting. War had rules and these people were done with rules. Why did they not simply lie down and accept Treotan? His people were not monsters, not tyrants. They would have roads, trains, lights, schools, administration, all the wonderful things other provinces already enjoyed. Unexpected delights. Clinics. Universities. Greenhouses. They could have *tomatoes in the winter*, godsdammit! What was so wrong with that?

At night, he sometimes went to the doorway— heavily guarded, so no one minded one tired, unarmed enemy near them—and looked down at the plain, where if there was enough moonlight coming through the mist, he could see the animals that kept the grass so bizarrely neat and short. Some kind of elephantine thing, but small, about the size of a sheep, with a long oval face ending in a circular mouth filled with what must have been very sharp teeth. From up here one could not see details, least of all in the unreliable light, but they came out in grayish herds, all together, and they ate the grass down till it was like velvet, and then they vanished again. Where? There was nowhere, nowhere at all in this landscape they could hide.

"What are they called?" he whispered one night to the guards, not expecting a response.

A pause. Then, "Those are *ust'ine*," one of them said, an old man, gruff and curt.

Tzajos thanked him, and crept back inside. Alyea was gone; he might get a few minutes' sleep. But he paused, seeing the interpreter still awake and sitting next to the pile of answers in Tzajos's writing, slowly going through the thick sheaf of paper. Not much blank paper was left. Did that mean they must bring more paper, or that Alyea had calculated how much she might need, and the questioning was almost done? It did not matter. He had no secrets now; he had told them everything. He had worked his way through all their pencils, his own pencil lead supply, and had switched to his fountain pen, and that too was running out of ink. He wondered how many pages he had left in him.

"What is happening here?" Tzajos said softly, sitting next to the interpreter. "Can you tell me?"

"They are making more recruits," Calamuk said, also keeping his voice low. "Find the places the war did not reach, and see who is left and who will fight. Then they will go to the camps and break everybody free."

"They're not *prisons*. It's hardly a matter of—"

"And then," Calamuk said, "they will expel the interim government, and Seudast will belong to ourselves again."

"*Why?*"

"I am done lecturing you," Calamuk said bleakly. "Nothing gets through. What do they do to you people over there? I am not asking this rhetorically. What do they *do* to the children in the schools, why are you all like this, why is it so hard to shift? The way you see the world, you think it's not just your right but your duty to take anything you think isn't being used to its full extent, that doesn't have every penny squeezed out of it.

"You see a man leading a horse along the road and you don't ask him why he's doing it, you are profoundly dead to the idea that maybe the horse is lame, or new to the saddle, or the man has just purchased it, or if he feels like walking... The *idea* of asking never even occurs to you. Why would it? All you see is a man and a horse and you think, *He's doing it wrong! Horses are for riding!* You don't say to him, 'In my country, we ride horses.' You don't even say, 'You *should* be riding that horse. You just snatch away the lead and you kick him into the ditch, and you say, 'If you can't use this horse properly, you don't deserve it. I will take it and put it to work. And maybe someday, if you do as I tell you, and never disobey me, and swear you'll never, ever lead it, that you'll never *waste* a horse, you can have a horse again.' And you do that to the *whole world*. I give up on you.""

Calamuk got up, replacing the pile of papers on the crate, neatening the edges. For a second Tzajos thought he would say more—send out one last parting shot —but the interpreter walked away into the darkness, and left him alone.

Tzajos sat back down on his crate and put his head in his hands, scratching absently at the bristles growing on his chin. They didn't let him shave here. Not to regulations. Those camps... What if it was true? He must go back and...and file an official protest, that was it. Then someone would investigate and... He wished Calamuk had not said that. Don't give up on me, Tzajos thought bleakly. *Please, don't say that. Do you know how many people in my life have said that? You had no way to know. Why did you say that?*

Even as he asked it, he knew it did not matter. It was hopeless. He would never write his book. Maybe someday, in the future, someone from the camps...

An official protest will do nothing, someone said inside him, or several someones. *To obey their rules is to succumb to their rules. We must all live outside of them. And make our own. To protect not only people but humanity.*

"That's what the camps are *for*," Tzajos protested quietly. "That's the humane solution. They can't possibly live in all those destroyed farms on the front. This is *better*."

No

No

No

No

He sighed. "Tell me, then," he invited them, glancing around in case anyone was listening. "Tell me what *you* think. What you've seen. I know she hasn't asked you everything yet. The wizard. Even if you hate me, you can tell me. Can you?"

Silence, silence and darkness, and then light fluttering red against his shut eyes: fire, bright and hot, a summer night and a small smokeless fire of dry wood, darkness, distant lights, the roar of water, then the thud and snap of rapids, unlike a liquid at all, like a river of stones, and someone was wrestling with him, cold hands, bony and cold, *the bones of the dead the bones of the dead*, voices crying out, a furious multitude, *Kill him! Show him what it means! Can we kill him?*

Tell him! Don't kill him!

They're close. I don't know how close. I'm so sorry I fought with you the night before I left. I meant to say

No I didn't I never meant to I meant to go to my grave with that argument still

sorry before I went. I don't know why I didn't. Please tell Mama I kept fifty-five dai and some change in a can sealed with white oilcloth in the roof of the chicken coop. It's for

Give it to

you and her now. We anchored platforms on the south face of Vorom and we shoot from there. I think we can win this. Maybe if we cannot

We cannot

No, we cannot

win this we can at least show the monsters what it means to say no as I think no one has ever said no to them. Mama it's bleeding and it won't stop bleeding and it's been three days. The doctor says not to worry and it will stop soon and I don't need an operation but I still

You are coming to us, you will join us

worry. It won't stop bleeding. Darling how cold is the soil how cold it is and how it grips me all over like you did just once like warm and too close to say I lov

Then it is the night and the day and you see through our eyes before we fought before we needed to fight

There it is, there it is. That's how they did it. It played before his eyes like the illustration in a book come to blazing life and he wanted to cry out with amazement but he could not. The summer night and the fire and all the fighting still in the future by a few minutes, and the Treotan soldiers attacking the mine, dressed in civvies, fooling no one, and the Seudast miners and security men bursting out, shocked, pursuing—seizing the horses, galloping, kicking through the fire and putting it out.

Was this the truth? Or a story the dead men were telling him? Somewhere far away and high up his hand reached for a fresh sheet of paper, one of the last, and his pen, his good pen, almost empty. What language might he write in, whose tongue could he use? He drew instead: lines, arrows. Who steered his hand?

Treotan retaliated for our perceived incursion into their territory, across the border, someone told him, a sad young voice, scholarly, prim. *However, they were the ones who attacked first, luring us over the border. Since that had just been declared an act of aggression, it was the simplest thing in the world to call us the aggressor. The truth was, as you know, that the empire wanted what we had, and when we did not trade it quickly enough, when we could not produce it fast enough, they simply took it. The mine was a pretext. The agreements were a pretext. They had been planning it. And it was so simple to write it in the newspapers. After all, the only witnesses left were from the empire.*

Who are you? Tzajos wrote on the page.

There are several of us, speaking to the dead. You took yours home. Ours remain here. And they listen.

You don't want to go home too?

We are home. We are in prison but we are home.

Tzajos rose, scraping back the wooden crate, the sound waking a few others. Enough light for him to see the gleaming gold buried in Valens's brown hair as the man got up, strode toward him. The room wasn't terribly big. It must have been hard to chip out even this space. Twenty paces, maybe twenty-five.

One last problem to solve. Tzajos did not think he had solved any of the others but perhaps he had, all unknown. Nothing was left but this. Prisoners existed inside him—he would not say they lived inside him but he could say they existed. He must set them free; he must not continue to be an accomplice to their jailer, he must give them to their rightful master, death. For him, the war has been linear, with a beginning and an end. For this country, it has been a cycle, neverending, grinding them beneath its wheel with each turn. Cycles could be broken. Then time would lay flat again, pointing into the future.

Valens sped up to a run, shouting to the others. Matches hissed. Lanterns flared. Hands reached, uncertainly, disbelieving, not close enough.

Tzajos drove his fountain pen into his throat.

"*You're* signing up?" His father ruffles his newspaper to straighten the pages before setting it down, focusing his rheumy, cruel eyes properly on his son. "Draft or no draft, they'll never take you, boy. Why would they?"

"That's up to them to decide, Father. If they want me or not."

"No one wants you. World's full of people like that. Waste of space. I suppose the army can use that, though." The paper goes back up with a snap. "Whole war's a waste, if you ask me."

Why has he signed up? This is the entirety of the memory: the kitchen, the dirty dishes, sunlight through the lace curtains. Not even his father as a whole but just the half of him above the table, and the newspaper. Fighting for honor and duty and the safety of our borders against those backward people who have decided they have a vendetta against us. Better than fighting over money.

Always Lyell Tzajos has been pushed around by others. That's fine too, his father says sometimes. Bullies are not doing anything more unnatural than predators and prey. Always he has done what he's told. Fine: in school there are rewards for that. In university, more yet. Prizes. Scholarships. The world is a box and if the box shrinks in size every year, Tzajos will still fit. He is neat, he is tucked-in. He folds. He does not think that the army will make a man out of him. He did think he would be given a bigger box. Then his name is on the blue form and they are taking his blood and measuring his chest. Still he is not thinking about killing for money even though that's what he will be asked to do.

And now he is dying. Not for money. For a lie. And to set free the truth.

He tries to say goodbye to his father, or the memory, or the newspaper. Maybe just the kitchen. He can say nothing. He is gone, leaving. There is nothing but light and the cry of voices around him, and a rushing sound over all of it, like the sea.

Dear Mariye,

Tzajos paused, and stared ahead of himself: the green grass, the flowers. He had no idea what day it was, and the spot in the letter where that was supposed to go seemed painfully blank. "Yather?"

"Yes, sir?" The captain appeared at his side, stooping solicitously. "Feeling all right, sir?"

"I'm fine... What day is it?"

"The seventeenth."

"Thank you." Tzajos gingerly touched the bandage around his throat, feeling nothing—there were too many layers between fingertips and skin. He couldn't even turn his head. He remembered dying; Yather said, matter-of-factly, that he *had* died, for perhaps as long as two or three minutes. And there had been, to hear it told, a perfect explosion of lights and a strange sound, like a wail of combined voices— "Like an orchestra tuning up," Garawe had said afterward. Tzajos had had no idea that Garawe liked orchestral performances, but now they discussed their favorites almost every day. What a strange world.

Tzajos tilted his writing board again and put the pencil back to the page.

I'm writing to say I will be back later than I initially indicated, which is to say, never. Unfortunately, if I return, I will be court-martialed and you will see me only in a state whose sight I would prefer you not endure: arrested or already imprisoned.

However, I think I have done as my conscience sees fit, whether our courts understand that or sympathize with it at all. Because it is not that the Dastians were too hurried or uncaring to mark their graves. They bury their dead as close to the spot of death as possible, and they <u>deliberately</u> did not mark them in this conflict, having learned previously that the enemy might return to defile them. Which we in this case did. Their greatest fear.

*Mariye, what I lacked I did not even know
I lacked. Not merely understanding. Perhaps a
human heart. Like the government of Treotan
(there: that is officially treason and it is in
writing, and I will sign it too).*

"That's a four."

"It is *not* a four."

"It *is* a four. You're reading it wrong."

"*You're* the one who can't read."

Tzajos blinked. "Language lessons going well, I see," he said to Yather.

"They're getting along like a house on fire, sir," Yather said contentedly, joining Tzajos on his rock. "I've noticed the numeracy is goin' a mite faster than the literacy, even though technically gambling is against regulations."

"Well, we're not in the army any more, so the regulations don't apply," Tzajos said. "And you don't have to call me sir."

"Old habits. Want a cup of tea?"

"If anyone's making." Tzajos listened to the card game-slash-language lesson in the background, then began to write again. It was strange how much easier it felt these days, how much lighter his hand felt. Perhaps it was simply losing so much blood before they had patched him up. Perhaps there really *was* less of him to haul around.

*Forget the mission. The markers of the
graves exist in the hearts of the survivors, and
that is where they wish to keep them. Using our
maps, the Dastians and my men are retracing*

our tracks to re-inter every set of remains and all of their effects where they were found. The stored teleplasm has been emptied into the atmosphere. It was quite something to see.

I cannot bring back the dead, nor can I, alone, free East Seudast from its new chains. But I have done what I can, as little as it is. I may die for it. I think that is all right. I have told all the men in my unit to do as they see fit—it is unlikely that a Deserters Response Special Unit will be sent for us. There simply are not enough men left to waste. And Treotan does hate waste.

I suspect that all of them will decide to stay here.

This is very strange to me.

I am sorry that I was not a better husband, Mariye. I am sorry I will not have the chance to redress my many wrongs toward you. I wish I could spend ten lifetimes treating you with the kindness you have always deserved and I rarely dispensed. I hope you will take some friends, or your new husband, and go to Banotin as you dreamed, for a good long holiday.

Cpt. Yather says it is beautiful. He sends his regards.

We have also a wizard here for some reason.

To end I will just say: the Dastians told us the mists would lift at winter's true end. And so they have. I am writing today under a clear blue sky, and everyone is outside ploughing their fields for first planting. The ice is gone from the soil. The chill has left the air. We will go with the sun behind us. I love you.

Your Ly.

THE WEIGHT OF
WHAT IS HOLLOW

Death came to the hanging all dressed in rags. Taya nodded to her, as one professional to another, and watched her vanish into a discreetly shadowed corner.

The crowd was not uniform; watchers had spaced themselves out as precisely as knots in a piece of lace. No one wanted to stand near a stranger. Taya and her aunt and cousin made a small, tight knot right at the front, behind the purple ribbon separating watchers from participants. Such was their family's prestige as the makers of the bone-gallows.

"Stop that," whispered Aunty Lasidu.

Taya put her slide rule back into her coat pocket. Sorry, sorry, yes of course—if you were seen fidgeting at these things it looked as if you were bored, and boredom was an insult to the tradition. And the tradition had faces, eyes, sabers, guns, and connections... There it was, in an unbroken line. Black uniforms, brass buttons, cold-reddened cheeks.

The officers wore fur hats adorned with the feathers of magpies, attached with colorful glass tiles indicating rank and division. Half-buried in the fur, they glittered like the eyes of wild animals. As usual, the soldiers were looking at the gallows, their expressions unguarded—full of revulsion and wonder. And as usual, the officers were looking at the crowd. Who had come? From which neighborhoods? What were their professions—were there students, guildsmen, tradies? Were there foreigners and therefore perhaps spies? Who looked disapproving or censorious or disgusted or overly gleeful?

"It's very good," Aunty Lasidu murmured, her breath pluming out, hiding her face. "The old styles are coming back. Did you note that, Tayavic?"

"Yes'm." In fact, Taya had barely registered the gallows, having determined at a glance that the build corresponded with her uncle's blueprints. She felt—had not quite calculated, but sensed—that the lengths and breadths and widths and weights were within acceptable tolerances. Details soothed her. She had grown up thinking everyone felt the same way about them and had only been disabused of the idea a few years ago. It did not change her essential nature.

Details, numbers, measurements, they were a comfort—they were a *relief*, the sensation no different to her mind than that of pouring cold water on a burn. When the numbers were right, the pain ceased. It was not happiness except that life seemed to burn her more often and more deeply than other people, and relief was close enough to happiness after a while.

The morning was cold and clear; frost glimmered in the shadows like ground glass. When the sun rose high enough to hit the ornamental sundial on the tower behind the gallows, they would begin. Taya hoped someone had told the prisoner that. Locals knew, but for foreigners it made the waiting easier; they were less likely to fight, protest, beg, attempt to escape.

Golden light slowly filled the square. Around her she heard people whispering with, she hoped, admiration, as the gallows began to glow—every femur, every rib, every tooth in every skull throwing back the light like polished brass.

There: a dot of sun on the gnomon. A colonel mounted the creaking steps, clinging tightly to the banister—bone was slippery to begin with, and the frost made it treacherous. The charges were contained on a single sheet of paper this time, brought from an ordinary envelope whose red wax seal he cracked with ease. Taya had seen hangings where the charges were written on a scroll as long as her arm. But today was easy. The prisoner was not a disgraced nobleman or fallen bureaucrat; he was just an enemy soldier, selected for hanging instead of beheading.

He agreed that he was guilty of the crime of fighting against the Treotan empire; he stood still as the soldiers dropped the noose around his neck and Taya's uncle checked the knot.

Everything was suffused with light; everyone moved through a thousand panes of amber glass, trailing silky scarves of breath. The colonel pulled on the ribboned lever, bone meeting bone in the mechanism below. The trap-door swung down in beautifully-engineered silence.

And the prisoner did not die.

Taya realized it first in her body—waves of heat despite the coldness of the morning, sweat bursting on her bare palms, the back of her neck, her forehead. The man was suffering—was strangling, his legs kicking, muscles convulsing, sounds coming from his body that she had never heard from a human being.

Aunty Lasidu said nothing, did not frown or gasp; only moved her hand to touch her daughter's elbow, surely not a motion large enough to attract the attention of the officers, who anyway were staring up at the ugly death. Taya looked at the faces of the officers and regretted it at once.

It seemed to go on forever. Taya watched till the end, till she felt the hanged man stamped on the back of her eyes—as if she had been staring at the sun. If it had been carried off properly it would have been over in those shining moments when the whole square was full of light. Now the passing minutes made it all dull again. Cold grey granite and the gallows no longer a thing of magical beauty but just the bones of a dozen corpses, death out of death, death creating death.

At last the noises stopped. Taya did not think the man was dead—close, but not quite. She waited for Aunty Lasidu to move, and then she took her cousin Vil's hand and followed her aunt out of the square and back to the carriage waiting on Sewaday Street. They did not look back at her uncle. His duties were not yet discharged.

TREATMENT

After the material has been defleshed as in previous section, it must be treated or it will be unsuitable for use.

Apprentices may believe that fresh bone is preferable to work with, as it is easier to cut the complex joints required for structural integrity. The ease is an illusion. Fresh bone is softer, which is the end of its list of virtues. If one constructs anything with fresh bone and allows it to dry, the mistake will be evident at once. Dried bone becomes unusably brittle and will not bear weight. It also shrinks (unevenly and unpredictably along all axes), torques, and bends (often up to tens of degrees off true). The color change from white to yellow/brown may also be undesirable.

The objective of treatment is to render the material strong rather than simply hard. More care will be required to mortise and tenon treated bone, and therefore more time, but this is a very small cost in comparison to the benefits.

Treatment should be immediate after defleshing except in the case of skulls if they are ornamental rather than structural. It is acceptable for decorative skulls to go untreated.

Equipment and quantities: see Diagram 18
- Pressure vessel (for cutaway view see Diagram 19)
- Valve cap
- Valve handle (detachable)
- Rubber mallet
- Water for pressure-filtered well water is acceptable provided there are no large particles visible
- Water for vessel — well water should be filtered through at least five layers of Thryban (grade: fine) before being brought to a rolling boil and boiled steadily for at least 20 minutes
- Awasse ash solution 10% strength in alcohol
- Qe-vesine resin 50% strength in water
- Serpent milfoil solution 1% in water — optional but has a strong whitening effect. At the time of this manual's writing, serpent milfoil is proving difficult to source due to the war

Taya hesitated, then scratched out *the war* and wrote *military operations*. Then she scratched out *due to military operations* and ended the sentence at *source*.

This too was like working on a gallows—the last steps, the polishing, because even if no one could see a splinter of bone, it could still be felt. And even if a normal hand would not feel it, her aunt's hand would.

For a long time she sat motionless at the desk, poised as if she were about to write again, the fine machine-made lead in her propelling-pencil still resting on the page. Her father's paper, one of a hundred pads of military-issue graph paper he had left the workshop when he died. Her father's good drafting pencil, bequeathed specifically to his only child. *May you use it all your life*, he had written, *with wisdom and honor.*

The manual had been his idea as well, suggested just before his death—ten years ago, but Taya had not felt prepared to begin till now, near the end of her apprenticeship, and Aunty Lasidu had agreed. A know-nothing can write nothing worth knowing, she'd said. May as well give it to one of the mill donkeys as to a green apprentice for all the use you'd get out of it.

At any rate, father and aunt had both agreed that someone needed to write down appropriate procedures; it was simply becoming untenable to let everything reside in people's heads. Worse yet, every gallows-maker in the family (Taya was discovering) had their own little idiosyncrasies, and while nothing had ended in disaster yet—the only disaster possible, a failed execution—there were too many contradictions, too many points of dissent, too many "suggestions" and "experiments."

Take this morning's failure as an example, which Aunty Lasidu had certainly spotted as well: the cracks in the gallows-arm when it had taken the weight of the prisoner, suggesting that her uncle had not treated that bone correctly. So: a gruesome asphyxiation rather than a broken neck. She had never seen that before. Things needed to be standardized.

They had agreed on that too: Taya would be good at standardization.

A scratch at the door: Vil, who never knocked, coming to get her for dinner. Taya let the girl in and said, "Five minutes," pointing at the chair next to the door. Vil sat and folded her hands in her skirt, and Taya returned to her desk to make a fair copy of what she had just completed.

This was another reason for the manual Aunty Lasidu's only daughter, who should have been apprenticed first, except that everyone agreed she was...unsuitable. That was the official ruling, which was something of a blessing, Taya always thought, given the host of other words they could have used. Vil could not or (Taya suspected) would not speak, she could not follow anything but the most simple of instructions, she had never learned to read or write, let alone manage the complex calculations required for the bone-gallows. She had trouble knowing where her hands and even her feet lay in terms of her surroundings; her knuckles were always black and blue from knocking into cabinets, tables, the edges of things. You'd feel nervous handing her the razor-sharp chisels or augers of their trade.

That little Vil, an infant of surpassing beauty and vigor, might break the line of hereditary apprenticeship was entirely unexpected but not a disaster—there were, as Aunty Lasidu used to say (grimly, repeatedly), other children. But one by one they had either proved unsuitable themselves, or gotten themselves killed in one or another war. They were running out of cousins. The adepts were getting older. Somebody had to write something down eventually; and eventually had become now.

Taya gathered up the fair copy. "Dinner?"

Vil gestured uneasily at her throat. At the gesture Taya felt something close off in her own throat, and she waited it out as one would a tremor in the hands—staring out the attic's small triangular windows at the trees below, a soft and rushing sea of crimson and bronze, hiding the roofs of the other houses on the street. She knew what her cousin meant. "That wasn't supposed to happen," she said. "I... It won't happen again."

Vil closed her eyes and put both hands to her throat—not squeezing, Taya sensed as she reflexively pulled her cousin's hands down, but holding tightly, as if to make a scarf of the flesh.

"It *won't*," Taya said again, unsure as always whether Vil understood her—whether they were even speaking of the same thing. "Come on, you've seen as many of these as I have. You *know* that doesn't happen. Just... forget about it, all right?"

She climbed down the ladder first, leading the way to the kitchen so that she could hold the door open for Vil, as was proper. Always younger for older, never older for younger, a tradition she kept even though she was barely a year younger than her cousin.

Inside, the long wooden table had been set for four; lamplight gleamed softly on the black claywork bowls and cups, the fire mostly banked under a simmering iron pot. Taya helped Aunty Lasidu fry and salt the last of the cseper, then piled the hot flatbreads on a tray. Uncle's absence was like a ghost in the room, palely hovering, expectant, sure someone would say something—could they not feel the uncanny chill he gave off?—but at her aunt's nod, Taya filled a bowl for him too and placed it at the head.

Mutton stew, not very surprisingly. This was the time of year for it, when farmers had to decide which of their animals they wanted to feed through the winter and which, bluntly, they did not. Vil began to push her bowl away—she didn't like meat—but before Taya could try to soothe her, Aunty Lasidu snapped, "You'll eat what's put in front of you or you won't eat at all. We've been through this. And you need proper nutrition. You're no wider than a chalkline." She turned. "Deliver the benediction, Tayavic."

Taya glanced at Uncle's empty seat and waited for her aunt to add something like *He'll be here*, but the pause stretched out, and finally she put her hands on either side of her bowl and recited her lines.

It didn't mean anything. He had probably gotten delayed; the sun was going down; it was mercilessly icy after the brief lunchtime drizzle had frozen on the cobbles; you couldn't rush in this kind of weather; sometimes you were dealing with medical officers that were new to the paperwork...

The first few bites were eaten in silence, broken by the occasional pop from the fire. When manners dictated she could talk again, Taya pushed the few sheets of paper over to her aunt. "The new section. It's not done yet."

Aunty Lasidu dabbed her mouth with a napkin and picked up the pages. Without looking up, she said, "Make her eat."

"Yes'm." Taya looked at the empty chair again as if it would make a difference, then forced her gaze away and tore up a csep for her cousin, pushing it below the surface with her spoon. "Can you eat a few of those?" she whispered.

"Do not present it as a choice, Tayavic. She's to do what she's told."

"I think it's the texture of meat that bothers her, Aunty. She'll...she'll get some of the goodness this way, surely. In the broth."

"This is good," Aunty Lasidu murmured as if Taya hadn't spoken, setting the pages aside. "Instead of 'water for pressure' and 'water for vessel,' I would suggest 'water for steam pressure,' then 'water for contents of vessel.' It should be obvious to a casual reader, but we want to remove all ambiguity. You should also add a few lines for the use of arduch-ard—I will give you the quantities after we finish the dishes."

"I don't know that one. What's it for?"

"Teeth and only teeth. It's very expensive, and I hear that the fish from which it's taken is becoming nigh-impossible to catch even in the south; but the manual should be thorough."

Taya nodded, glanced at her cousin, glanced back at the sheets, took another piece of bread. "I thought I should also add something," she began through the lump in her throat, "about...modifying treatment for cold temperature...to prevent mistakes. Unnecessary cruelty. To the...uh, the users..."

A stony silence. In it Taya seemed to hear the pressure vessel getting up to steam, the water getting hotter and hotter and more and more angry at its captivity. At once she regretted opening her mouth, even though she hadn't mentioned the cracked bone from the morning. Whether it had been Uncle's error in choosing the bones, treating them, joining them, or simply sheer bad luck, she had no right to criticize him even indirectly.

"Cruelty is not a word we recognize," Aunty Lasidu said tonelessly. "Justice must be done, and it is not handed out by those in our position. We speak only of the work. Not of its outcomes. Are we clear?"

"Yes'm."

"You may add the cold-weather modifications to the text," she went on, returning to her stew. "The work does not respect season. Better to be prepared."

Vil looked up sharply, staring at the door; Taya knew what this foretold, and she respectfully put her spoon and bread down, and wiped her fingers clean of lingering oil and salt. A minute later the door opened, revealing her uncle, finely dusted in snow that vanished as he stepped inside—and three soldiers.

Instinctively Taya searched her memory for the filed details: yes, all three had been at the hanging. A colonel flanked by two young lieutenants, both boys tall, gangling, careful not to block their superior's view. The colonel's face pale and unsmiling under dark hair. Lips white as bone.

Uncle offered food, accepted their refusal, offered seating, was refused again, remained standing, as they all did. Taya resisted staring at him with an effort. What was happening? She could not recall officers ever coming to the house after a hanging, not the big men who actually commissioned the gallows. Sometimes they would send couriers to tap on the door with corrected or misplaced forms—receipts or certificates, things like that. As often as not they would push the paperwork through the letter-flap and leave.

The colonel studied each of them in turn, apparently feeling no urge to fill the silence as Uncle did. Vil, silent and trembling, her eyes huge; Aunty Lasidu, a wooden statue carved in beautiful detail, still holding a wooden spoon. Uncle red and sweating, as if he had not ridden here in the carriage but run behind it. Taya last and longest.

"I will be brief," the colonel said in his clipped, brittle accent. "I am Colonel Gerhach; my current commission is attached to the Department of Justice. I deal exclusively with military prisoners—internal and external. At this current time: primarily prisoners of war. Naturally my duties are not unilateral." The white lips compressed; Taya thought he had attempted a smile. He went on, "The committee to which I report was present at this morning's execution. Opinions were...mixed."

Uncle blanched, his brick-red face visibly draining of blood. Taya's ears were ringing. Had they come because they had been appalled by the morning's execution? Was her uncle to be flogged? Imprisoned? Worse? In the long silence she convinced herself that the purpose of this visit was to commission her uncle one last time: to build his own gallows.

Gerhach turned to Taya. "You," he said. "You are the bone-gallows apprentice, yes? What's your name?"

"Yes, sir." She took a deep breath and tried again, this time actually speaking aloud. "Yes, sir. I am my aunt's apprentice. Tayavic."

"Not his?"

"No, sir. My cousin was apprenticed but he passed away." Taya kept her eyes on the colonel's chest, hoping her eyes were averted enough to be respectful. It was better to not look at his face.

"In general," Gerhach said, "tradition would dictate commissioning the most experienced maker available for each execution. *But* there is no regulation, no policy, no guideline. Nothing is written. I have...some leeway. And I have decided that you, Tayavic the apprentice, will build the next gallows."

He snapped his gloved fingers at one lieutenant, producing an almost inaudible *toc*, and handed Taya the paperwork. She accepted it in numb fingers. How many of these thick white envelopes had she held? How many seals had her father let her snap, knowing she liked the sound of the wax? And all those miles of purple ribbon she had been allowed to keep... Of course, apprenticeships ended with an envelope of one's own, but it still felt unreal.

Aunty Lasidu said, "With all due respect, Colonel, the girl has not completed her apprenticeship. She is seventeen; she has more than a year before she can receive her stamp. However, if you are dissatisfied with my husband's gallows, I myself—"

"Your craft secrets are none of my concern," Gerhach said dismissively. "Accepting the work is. Do you accept?"

Taya blinked. She had never heard of anyone rejecting a gallows commission—had never even considered it possible. The work was like rain, falling and ceasing for reasons unfathomable even to the gods.

Aunty Lasidu said, "She accepts."

"Very good."

The lieutenants filed reluctantly out of the warmth; Taya heard as if from a great distance, even though it was only a few paces away, one of them clucking to the horses. Gerhach paused at the threshold, surrounded for a moment by the feathery breath of the warm kitchen as it escaped into the cold outside. "I have been informed that...a repeat of this morning's execution would not go amiss," he said flatly. "Among certain Committee members."

And then they were gone, leaving only a chill in the room, as if their ghosts had remained to listen.

ACQUISITION OF MATERIAL

In the earliest days, animal bones were used at the request of the commissioning officers—at that time, mainly the royal court and a small number of the wealthier warlords. In part this was due to ease of supply, which meant minimal time between request and use. There were at least eight and perhaps as many as ten families who possessed the relevant knowledge and expertise. Since the work made them more wealthy than other families, they were often able to provide the bones of oxen, goats, sheep, and (occasionally) horses from their own tables. At this time only the wealthy would have been able to provide these bones.

In part the request was also due to a belief that hanging was an ignominious death — so while the spectacle and beauty of the gallows was for the spectators, the victim would only know that their death was taking place on, essentially, waste. It was intended to be an insult.

Currently, with just one remaining family qualified to build bone-gallows, the tradition has shifted toward using human bone exclusively. The tradition is also considered to be

---

Taya hesitated. Her father had never told her why the shift had been made; neither had anyone else. If she couldn't explain the historical reasoning, why bother putting it in? Aunty Lasidu would cross this all out. It was irrelevant to the acquisition of the bones.

Instead of crossing it out, she tore off the page and started a new one.

ACQUISITION OF MATERIAL

Apprentices are not permitted to acquire material without an Adept present. Only an Adept can sign for the material from the Mortuary and Interment Office, and they must present a valid family stamp so that an impression may be taken for the receipt.

It is very important to provide the MIO with the names of graduating apprentices immediately post-ceremony so that records may be kept current. Otherwise, verification of identity may take from days to weeks, depending on administrative requirements, which obviously delays commissions to a corresponding degree.

The MIO will provide the Adept and any assistants/apprentices with the required material in wooden boxes. These remain property of the MIO and must be returned after

---

Taya sighed and scribbled out *depending on administrative requirements*. Working on the manual had been reassuring, familiar, simply removing the various books in her head about this section or that and putting them onto the shelf of the paper. She had been going to the MIO with her father, her uncle, or Aunty Lasidu since before she could see over the top of the counter. Old Mr. Burkin still seemed to think she was that little pair of eyes, and always gave her a piece of candy when she came in, even though she was taller than Aunty Lasidu now.

But nothing felt familiar, nothing felt safe. She pushed the pad away and picked up the thick white envelope again, broke the wax seal, gently unwound the ribbon.

It was not an unusual commission. The prisoner this time was a deserter—that was surprising, and she kept reading. Ah, an officer. Deserters were usually flogged and reinstated, occasionally imprisoned. But you could certainly die for trying to take men with you, or for being a leader of men and leaving. Approximate height, approximate weight at time of capture—you had to reduce that by twenty percent if he was in the regular prison, eight or ten percent if he was in the fancy one attached to the courthouse, where he no doubt was being held. His execution was scheduled for two weeks from now. That was normal. There was nothing she needed to take into account for this gallows, except...except...

She thought about last night, the quietly unsettling conversation over their cooling food. So far from being either angry or insulted, relieved or irritated, everyone had just seemed...dazed. As if they had all been struck a tremendous blow on the head and were waiting for sense to return.

"You can build it for her, Las," her uncle had said. His voice had been perfectly steady, the only sign of his nervousness the piece of bread he was tearing to pieces in his thick, cold-swollen fingers. "No one needs to know. She can bring it in like normal and..."

Aunty Lasidu frowning, her mouth a straight line. "You're as much a fool as she is," she snapped. "You didn't see his eyes on her? Just now or this morning?

He'll be back. He'll pretend it's an audit, an inspection, something—he'll pretend he forgot something at the house, or he'll ask to change the paperwork, or something. And it'll be her that has to deal with it. You'll see."

"What?"

"Don't let the uniform knock the sense out of you. It's no more than a cloak thrown over a boar ready for the rut."

"What?" Uncle said again, then shook his head. "Not our Taya!" He paused, then added, as an afterthought, with an extra edge of anger, "And she's underage, anyway!"

Not our Taya. No, she hadn't seen what her aunt was talking about—not even a hint of it, not a whiff. As far as she had perceived in the brief meeting in the kitchen, Gerhach had wavered somewhere between sincere contempt for the whole sordid business of "building things" and actual loathing.

Lasidu turned to her. "Eat your food," she said, surprising Taya. "I'll help you as much as is allowed. Tonight, you need to go to bed with a full belly and clean teeth, and you need a night's sleep. In the morning we'll begin. And may the gods help us all."

May they help us all kill a man in the way we are being paid to kill him...

Taya blinked, dazed; she had been staring at the window and her eyes refocused only reluctantly. She had dreamed of being utterly alone, of standing on a pinnacle of rock surrounded by a night sky that rushed and sighed like the ocean, pierced by stars white-hot and close enough to touch, and no one else in the world, no one living or dead anywhere.

After breakfast they must take the carriage downtown to the MIO, and then the rest of the day would be spent over the big drafting table in the workshop. She nudged the envelope aside and touched the guardians of her desk: compass, pencils, rulers, slide-rule, corrective fluid, ink-bottle, the beautifully-embossed silver box containing extra pencil leads. A strange cityscape rendered in fanatical detail, as if tapped out with a blunted needle. With such things had her father built things that killed. With such things would she as well. But not like that, surely...

Yes like that. Yes in any way we are told. What difference does it make?

She folded the ribbons, put them in the drawer, and went downstairs to help cook breakfast.

DESIGN CONSIDERATIONS

In some cases, the Letter of Commission will request specific design elements. In cases where these requests are physically impossible (for example, insufficiently weightbearing), the officer must be contacted at once and the deficiency explained so that the letter can be modified and a modification initialed.

If no design is suggested, the best place to start is the Plan Archive (currently kept in the East wall of the workshop in the green-painted cabinet). However, it is expected that each gallows will be unique. The officers who adhere to this particular tradition have long memories, often make notes or drawings from life, and are not pleased with repeated designs.

Not pleased? Disapproving? No, neither was quite right to capture the level of polite but frozen disdain.

It was the morning of the fourth day. She did not have time to work on her manual; she must, as the other mornings, quickly eat, then go down to the workshop and start up the fire. The treatment vessel would also have had the night to depressurize; she must make sure the treatment worked and check the exterior locks. On the streetcorners they had begun seeing a strange thing: clusters of people, most only a little older than she, holding up signs protesting the war. When the city watch approached they split up, nimbly, like mice, and vanished. They had not covered their faces; they showed them defiantly, as if daring the watch to identify them again later. Their faces were red with anger and daring and frost, the whites showing in their eyes like frightened horses. What were they hoping to accomplish out there, with their flimsy card-board signs against the might of the government and the army? It was very strange.

The front was very far away, but, like death, the war was everywhere; it was in the air like smoke, on the ground like frost. When Taya ate her porridge war was there at the bottom of the bowl. It was in the metal canister that held their almonds. It was in the silver cityscape of her father's lead-holder, and it was in the leads themselves.

It was inside the workshop, as she went to unlock the big sliding doors and jumped when Gerhach stepped out from a darkened corner between the brick walls. "Sir," she said, and made a little bow before stooping to paw up the key-ring from the cobbles with her mittened hand.

"I have come to observe the progress," the colonel said brightly. "To report back to my superiors."

"It is early days yet, sir," Taya mumbled. "We have ten days before—"

"I will inspect the worksite when I like, as often as I like. Open the door."

Inside, Taya stoked the fire back to life and opened the shutters, admitting dawn's milky light on three sides. The treatment vessel was cold, the pressure gauge reading zero; the pale blue sheet laid in the catchment tray remained pale blue, no dark spots indicating leakage.

At Gerhach's prodding, Taya explained each step and each piece of equipment: the cart wheeled back out of storage, the lever that engaged the locks, the clips that attached it to the door of the treatment vessel. Opened, the vessel breathed out its sharp miasma of resin and acid. She wished Aunty Lasidu was here. Surely she must come in soon. Please, please, soon. The treated bones removed with padded tongs, placed on the cart, transferred to the big metal table for rinsing and inspection. The special spirit-lamp and filter that gave a clear white light, the thick magnifying lens brought all the way from Sabhelm more than fifty years ago.

Gerhach picked up the red grease-pencil dangling from the table on its delicate length of chain. "What is this?"

"For circling defects. The apprentice normally does that. Then the Adept inspects the defects. If they are large, they will usually have to be cut out, or the whole bone discarded. If they are small, sometimes we can patch them with putty, or change the design to use the piece somewhere that it won't bear weight. It's not true that a broken bone is stronger where the break has healed. The broken place is much more likely to break again. Always."

Gerhach replaced the pencil and put his hands behind his back, wandering the perimeter of the workshop. "And this?"

"That's the incinerator."

"What do you incinerate in it?"

She stared at him for too long; she knew it was too long even before he turned and met her gaze. He was still wearing his uniform cap, and in the shadow that masked the top of his face she could still see his eyes, not blue, not grey, not a human color at all in the faint light but silver as a spoon. "Waste material," she said.

"Flesh," he said. The word sounded terrible in his accent, as if he had never said it before—as if he had never needed to say it before. "From the...bones."

"Yes." *What else would it be from?* she almost said, but waited in silence for his next question, wrenching her eyes firmly down to the floor. *And how else were you supposed to get rid of it? Defleshing took a long time. You could not have it cluttering up the workshop, attracting vermin. Burning was clean and quick. There was a filter for the smoke. It was asking a lot of the neighbors to have the ash fall on their vegetable gardens and their clean washing.*

Aunty Lasidu bustled in, hesitating only a moment when she saw Gerhach, then confidently—Taya felt as if she were watching the older woman step into a costume which she had only just removed—assumed the role of Adept, offering to answer *any* questions the good colonel might have that her very *young*, remember, her very young and *not* actually certified apprentice might have mistakenly attempted to answer.

Gerhach left, his bootheels clacking on the stone outside for a long time—too long, Taya thought. As if his carriage was waiting all the way down the block, instead of near the house.

"You didn't believe me before," Aunty Lasidu said when the sound finally faded. "His interest in you."

"It wasn't that I didn't believe *you*, it's just..."

Aunty Lasidu's face softened. "No, I see. It's that it's hard to believe."

Taya nodded. "*Him*."

"I know. Let's take a look at these."

Together they bent over the first batch of bones on the metal table, gleaming and white as porcelain, harder than oak. "He will be watching the operation very closely," Aunty Lasidu said quietly. "You know that."

"Yes, I know."

"I ask because I looked at your plans again. And it seems to me you have designed it in a way that..." Aunty Lasidu hesitated uncharacteristically. "Will not...satisfy his request."

Taya held still while her face flooded with blood, while her heart raced, stalled, raced. Later she would think she should have waited another moment, seized her instincts by the scruff of the neck instead of speaking at once after that first blush of discovery and shame. "The commission letter doesn't say anything about the design. It's my choice."

"It is not your choice, fool." Aunty Lasidu pushed the lens away and seized Taya's chin in her hand, something she hadn't done in years, something she had done to both Taya and Vil when she suspected she was not being closely attended.

And Taya responded precisely as she used to: letting her arms go limp, staring directly into Aunty Lasidu's eyes even though it filled her with inexplicable, crackling terror.

"I do not need you to look at our neighbors," Aunty Lasidu said, as Taya blinked at the apparent non sequitur. "Do I? Good. You already know our house is the biggest on this block. You know we are the only ones for many houses around—perhaps in the entire neighborhood— where we each get our own bed and our own room. Do you think they live like this? Hmm? Do you think they always have hot food on the table, do you think they have wood for the fire, new dresses every year, good leather shoes? Do you think they each have their own bed? Feather coverlets? No. They live like animals—they are always a day from death. And we are not. And the reason we are not is because we do what we are told and we do not argue technicalities.

"Do you truly believe that when you disobey Gerhach—when he sees that bastard's neck snap instead of watching him twist on the rope—no, don't move, *look at me*, little fool—do you truly believe that the other officers will look kindly upon him? Or that he will then look kindly upon you, upon any of us? Perhaps you think that we are in some way invulnerable because we are the only ones who can build the bone-gallows. You think that protects us? Stop squirming. Do you think that?

"Well, let me tell you right now: you are wrong. They can impoverish us, and they will. They can punish us, and they will. They can kill us, and they will. It will likely not be you or me, likely not someone who does the building. It will be someone else in the family—someone who will know that it was you who did this. Someone... expendable. She may even forgive you, because she will not know what is happening to her."

Vil. Taya stopped moving, and stared at Aunty Lasidu, frozen in terror. *They wouldn't*—yes they would. Why wouldn't they? At the best of times, the army was given its head to terrorize and abuse anyone they pleased. During a war they attained the status of gods. One might pray to them, but one could not expect clemency; mere mortals existed only for their use. And if you were not useful you should make yourself invisible—because it was better to suffer in silence than to attract their notice to your lack of utility. Gods did not like dead weight. They also did not suffer disobedience gladly.

Aunty Lasidu removed her hand; Taya, after a long pause, managed to breathe again.

"I'll re-do the plans," Taya said, because it was all she could say. "I'm sorry they were not satisfactory, Aunty."

"Good. Then I will again inspect them, and we will go on as before."

———

They ran out of qe-vesine; to Taya's surprise, it was her uncle who suggested sending Taya out to the old family property for more. As he spoke, Taya felt as if something was building up in the air above his head, and Aunty Lasidu's head too, heavy and real, bearing messages that only they could read—and that Taya knew she should be able to as well, but couldn't. Now and then Vil even looked up, as if she sensed it too. Like a stormcloud shaped like an old galleon, its sails bellied with salt wind, that big.

"Even with train fare," Uncle said, "it won't cost more than having the old man mail it to us. And then those clumsy apes in the post office—how do we know they won't break the bottles? Or worse, steal it to re-sell to us!"

Aunty Lasidu nodded, glanced at Taya, nodded again.

"And he's not getting any younger," Uncle went on. "Maybe he can't even make it to the post office any more. And..."

"And he hasn't seen Taya since she was a little girl," Aunty Lasidu said slowly. "He'd like to hear how we're doing. I'm sure."

Like the commission itself, it was not a matter of agreeing; Taya was more aware of it now, more aware that all her life had been a series of being pushed through doorways rather than choosing one to go through, but even though she found the timing strange, she did not mind. She had been leaving the city now and then to buy supplies or bring back equipment for a few years, although always accompanied by Aunty Lasidu. But it was reasonable to expect an Adept to go alone; only apprentices should need an escort.

For all her aunt's talk of their prosperity, Taya was still instructed to buy tickets for the second-class carriages, not first; she rode to Kabiq Station in a half-empty car, studying the skeletons of her fellow passengers from under her half-closed lashes (no one disturbed a sleeping girl), secretly pleased to have the opportunity to gather more details for her files.

That old man had lived through too many wars to be useful; his legs were visibly bowed from childhood rickets and the other bones would be weakened even if they looked sound. The two ladies across from her in their coordinated pink and brown dresses were promising, except that one of them was with child, and her bones wouldn't ever be as strong as before she had conceived, whether this was her first or her fifteenth.

A young man near the door with freshly scabbed wounds, skin flayed from his face in some recent, gruesome accident—no, in battle, she could see the blue medal on his lapel—had a stunningly beautiful, absolutely symmetrical skull with splendid doming, as she saw when he removed his hat to scratch at his cropped blond hair. It was strange that he kept trying to cover his face with his scarf and pull his hat so low, when he had a skull like that.

At the station she debated hailing a cabriolet, but on second thought decided against it; she had not been given much play-money for the journey, for one thing, and for another the flimsy city cab wheels were meant for travel on paved streets; they would never get her to Grandfather Etzim's house. She slung her satchel crossways across her body, as her father used to do, and began to walk.

Vesine trees kept most of their small, flat leaves until spring, and in autumn instead of changing to the bright scarlets and ambers and golds of other trees, they seemed to turn grey—an illusion caused by the flesh of the leaves vanishing from the veins, leaving delicate skeletons, white against the black bark. In spring they would fall all at once, burying the trunks hip deep, before putting out fresh leaves of green. Taya walked up the final path to the house, the occasional white leaf patting her face or hair like a questing butterfly.

Grandfather was waiting at the door, a big old man still—all Aunty Lasidu's side were tall. He had kept most of his hair, though the red had become white. "I heard the gate," he said, before she could greet him. "Come inside. Have some tea."

This meant make the tea, as it turned out; Taya wasn't surprised, and shed her coat and bag onto the chair near the door before heading to his big odousi, ancient and rust-spotted but still sound. Empty, of course. She stifled a sigh and went back outside to get water from the well.

"Las wrote to me." Grandfather gestured at the letter still on the table, written in a large, confident hand to make it easy on old eyes, marked already with a couple of brown tea rings. "Said you came to get more resin. You ran out."

"We didn't," Taya said, setting out cups and spoons. "We never *run out*. I checked before I left. I'm very careful."

He nodded. In the long silence neither of them felt like filling, she brewed tea, filled cups, unloaded the bread and cakes that Aunty Lasidu had sent. Up here there was no sound of horse-traffic, the endless clatter of wheels on cobbles, the roar of manufactory or endless whine of street commerce; she paused and listened, smiling, to the sound of the wind in the orchard. She had not been here for years—not since she was seven or eight—and while she recognized the awkward diffidence she felt for her grandfather as shyness rather than respect, she felt no disconnect from the place itself. It felt as familiar and beloved as her own bedroom.

They drank their tea; Grandfather ate two cherry-cakes. Taya nibbled the edge of one so that he would not eat alone, and when he was done, she said, "Aunty

Lasidu said I should ask you to...to look at my plans. I mean, check them over."

"Hm. Been a few years. See what I can see though."

She unfolded the flimsy paper of the copy, trying to avoid new tea rings on it, watching resignedly as one formed right in the middle anyway. She hadn't seen it on the table. Grandfather seemed to not notice; he sent her upstairs to get his magnifying glass from his bedroom, and spent perhaps half an hour reviewing the plans, unspeaking, his nose a few inches from the paper. He waved her away when she offered him a red pencil from her satchel.

"Looks all right to me," he finally said, sitting back down. "Not too flashy. Economical on material. Not seein' any weight-bearing flaws. Obviously apprentice work but I'd put my stamp on it, if it were mine."

"And this one?" She unfolded the revised plans that Aunty Lasidu had approved, and put them on top.

This time he took a single glance, not bothering with the magnifying glass, and shook his head. "Close, but not quite. That gibbet-arm don't look sound to me. It'll bow, but because of the rib strut here, it won't break so you can take him back up and start over. Can't hang a man with that. He'll suffocate instead. I'd re-work everything from the base of the arm on up."

Taya swallowed, hearing her suddenly dry throat click in the silence. "Grandfather..."

"Mm?"

It was easier to talk while they walked, and between his bad leg and the slope, she was able to explain everything between the house and the orchard gate. The old man listened, cocked his head at the name of the colonel, sucked his teeth for a moment as Taya described the commission and the absence of any specifications for torture before death.

"No," Grandfather grunted.

"I...what?"

"Open the gate. Can't get the latch any more."

Taya went on tiptoe to reach over the wooden gate, and thumbed the latch down. Inside the orchard, the ranked rows of spiral trunks rose glittering and dark into the blue sky, like charcoal sketches of themselves, each bearing its own cloud of green-turning-white leaves and eight or ten spiles hammered into the wood, following the twist like a staircase. Most of the buckets had less than an inch of the pale lilac-colored resin at the bottom; the nice thing about qe-vesine was that it flowed so slowly that you didn't have to worry about emptying the buckets more than once a month or so, even in the spring.

Grandfather unhooked a bucket and held it out to Taya, tilting it so she could see the sluggish movement of the thick liquid at the bottom, inhale its acrid, herbal smell. "No," he said again, in the same gruff tone. "If that's what the colonel said then that's what you'll give him. I guess that first set of plans you showed me was your original, hm? And the second one was what Las approved."

"Yes, Grandfather."

"You listen to her." He set the bucket on the ground and sat down heavily next to it on one of the thick protruding roots, folding his arms over his knees. A fallen leaf blew against his hair and vanished into the white. Taya remained standing, feeling near tears. In truth she had never expected him to... what, support her unorthodoxy? Suggest she go against the wishes of the colonel? But at least some sort of acknowledgement of what a terrible thing she had been asked to do. Because it *was* terrible, and it was worse that no one else seemed to think it was.

"You, I always thought were the bright one," he murmured, reaching out to touch the handle of the bucket, drawing his hand back. "Not like the other little one—can't remember her name. Always thought there weren't no oil in that girl's lamp."

"Vilamelitsa. Vil."

"Listen," he said. "I want you to look at these trees. I didn't plant these. These were planted five hundred years ago—maybe more. In the old country. You hear us talk about it? Well, it's not a place we left and could ever return to. It's not a place we can send our apprentices to get trained. It's right where we are, right where you're standing. After the Treotan rolled over us the lines on the map was erased and redrawn and suddenly we were in the middle of them. Not even a province with a name. They killed those of us that fought back—which is to say most of us. Three out of four families died without even a gravestone. Those of us that are left are alive because they spared us. Because we said: *We'll be like you. That's what you want. And what we want is to live.* They never had the touch for the bone-gallows; but they liked the look of it. They like the...the show. So we are allowed to live. When you see a vesine tree you know that's where we once lived. And you are alive to see it now and know that. Do you understand me?"

Taya nodded, unable to speak. The grief that silenced her felt like something external—as if she had been poisoned, as if the poison were contained in a nut or seed still lodged in her throat.

"Las is right." Grandfather got up slowly, bracing himself on the trunk, and picked up the bucket again. "It won't be you they come after, it won't be her. It's a waste. Sound of it, it'll be Rupaj—him they can spare—or their kid. Vil. Her because she's one of the few kids left, so that'll be a blow to us all, even if she never builds a thing."

"I love her," Taya managed, allowing the tears to finally fall, feeling them loosen the lump that blocked her airway.

"You love her even though she's useless? Well, they'll turn that in your hand like a blunted chisel," he said flatly. "They only love what's useful. Love has to be earned and it has to be earned again and again and again, because people forget. That's how we've survived this long. You remember that, you'll be all right. Out of all the peoples that Treotan has conquered—out of all the lands they've invaded—they let us live. *Us*. At any minute they can turn around and wipe us clean from the land, from memory, from their history books. They've done it to others before. So." He slapped one big hand on his thigh and handed her the bucket. "Hang that back up. Listen to Las. Don't kick up a ruckus for our whole family just to spare some stranger a single minute of pain. It's not worth it. The math won't work out in the end, Taya."

DESIGN CONSIDERATIONS

The world is a cruel place. We cannot be the only soft thing in it. The only thing we can do is strive to be merciful in our particular cruelty.

———————

Taya ripped out the page and crumpled it into a ball. Behind her the door opened in silence; she didn't turn.

"Well?" Aunty Lasidu said.

"Grandfather Etzim said the second set of plans were fine for the purpose."

"Good. I thought he might."

A long pause. Taya stared at the blank sheet of paper.

Aunty Lasidu said, "Did you talk about anything else?"

"No," Taya said. "He said I should listen to you. And do what I'm told."

"Good. I'll see you in the morning."

"Yes'm."

The door closed. Taya squeezed the ball of paper in her hand, harder, harder, till it dug into her flesh, imagining it turning into a diamond. The old man had sent her back with a pillow-sized bag of the dried resin, enough to get them through a decade of deserters, and had told her again, as she stood at the gate, to keep her head down and her hands on her work. It wasn't about cruelty, he said, just as Aunty Las had said. The regime were the cruel ones, not the makers of the gallows. War was the cruel thing; and to be hanged was a better death than they'd get on the front lines. Cruelty was what the family would learn firsthand if she failed them. She must please this colonel and keep her opinions to herself.

Can you do that for me? he said. *Tayavic? Look at me.*

Yes, Grandfather.

He looked so much like Aunty Lasidu, so much like Taya's own mother—the same strong nose, the shape of the eyes, the color like vesine leaves in spring with that dark green ring around them exactly the same. He was them and they were her and she must, *must* do what the family expected of her. No argument because no choice. She lived in a choiceless enclave, in a land where others had a choice.

Was it normal, did other people feel this way, did every subject of every empire go to sleep at night thinking *I am afraid of the people who run my country*, did they think *I fear my state*? Grandfather said it was about duty, not fear. But both were her masters. She served one if she served the other. *Neither* was not an option.

Taya opened her hand and looked at the ball of paper, small and grey from her sweat, like a piece of lead shot.

––––––––––

The deserter was not a young man, but Taya hadn't been expecting one. This often surprised people who were not so involved in the war—it "should" be the young men who fled, frightened by their first taste of combat, people thought. Not so. It was usually men like this, middle-aged, who had established a life outside of the training yard. A wife or a husband, children, a farm, elderly parents that needed tending... a weight you carried whenever you charged the enemy. Eventually some of them decided that the weight was not the problem, but the enemy was.

He was black-haired, handsome in a slightly scuffed or weathered way, his face sprayed with tiny white scars like flecks of ice. Taya passed him with only a single glance, meeting his eyes—dark brown, like tea—trying to say *I'm sorry* with the flick of her gaze and hoping from his she could perceive at least *It had to be this way*, since it would never contain *I forgive you for your part in this.*

For the first time she stood next to the gallows, inside the purple ribbon instead of outside, looking out at the crowd. Her eyes burned with exhaustion and the dry air; her muscles screamed with pain. Normally an Adept and an apprentice would set up together the night before, but with Taya playing the role of Adept, she'd had to go alone.

Nine hours in the dark, lit by a handful of oil lamps—this neighborhood had not yet been fitted for gas—assembling the elaborate puzzle of joints and angles, mortises and tenons, delicately tapping in the finger-bones carved to take the place of nails and screws, and every painstaking connection slowed to a maddening degree by the need for gloves in the autumn cold. She had barely had time to come home, bathe and change, hurriedly drink a cup of tea, and have Aunty Lasidu braid her hair before she ran out again. The horses had not even had time for their sweat to dry.

Aunty Lasidu, Uncle, and Vil stood in the front row as normal. Vil was pale, swaying; the dark circles under her eyes looked painted on with ink. Aunty Lasidu's face was stone, but Taya thought she could discern something almost like grim approval. The gallows was beautiful, sparkling with frost in the grey light of morning; Taya had added extra skulls for decoration, and painstakingly adhered rows of teeth like the sugar pearls on a wedding cake. It appeared majestic, overwhelming, even though it was just ten steps up instead of the usual five, not that much higher.

Gerhach appeared next to her, reeking of some heavy cologne, musky as an old fur coat. "Very impressive," he murmured. "For your first attempt."

"It's nothing, sir." She stared directly ahead, the crowd blurring into an indistinct mass the color of wet stone. People were still filing into the square, bumping one another, whispering *Excuse me, excuse me.* "It is my aunt's excellent training that you see." She felt a slight pressure on the back of her arm—his fingers, she knew without looking. For several seconds she waited for him to finish whatever it was this preliminary touch forewarned, but another officer was approaching them, and he turned away to speak to the man.

The charges were read; she studied the faces of the officers again, as before. A hunger in them, indecent. Some even licking their lips. Last time had been a pleasant surprise; now, having tasted the dish of this particular suffering, they salivated for more. Taya put her hands in her pockets and stood very still, back straight, letting them see her too—trying to will them, with her mind, to look at her instead of at the deserter who now climbed the steps. But she had become invisible to them—just a stray tool, like a dropped hammer, beneath the magnificent platform.

Again the light, falling into the stone square pink and translucent as a rose petal. Gerhach was gesturing to her; she climbed the bone steps, one hand on the railing, one hand hitching her skirt up so it wouldn't tangle.

Down went the noose; she touched the knot she had tied last night, making sure it was still correct and sat snug against the man's pale, jail-grimed neck. Gerhach hovered, as if even now he suspected her of unorthodoxy, as if she might whisper something to the prisoner—implicate herself in some conspiracy, some anti-establishment sedition, since they stood so close together.

Taya said nothing. The knot was good. She stepped backward, bowed to the waiting crowd, and nodded at Gerhach, who seized the lever with indecorous pleasure.

The trap snapped; the platform vanished under the deserter's boots. Unlike the sound of the mechanism, the sound of his neck breaking did not echo, muffled as it was inside his flesh.

Taya did not smile, did not move, did nothing for a full quarter of an hour until the medical examiners confirmed the death and allowed her to climb down to sign the certificate. Had there been a sound when he fell? A kind of sigh from the crowd? No, she must have imagined it. No one would dare.

Gerhach awaited her at the bottom, his face a mask of anger, visibly smoothing it out as Taya stepped down from the last stair and looked at him: meeting his eyes at last, measuring the height and weight of him, imagining his neck snapping too. That tiny sound! The sound of mercy, if nothing else. No, not sedition, not rebellion. Nothing so grand. Only Taya, alone, staring down the entire face of the empire in a courtyard blooming with rosy light.

He broke first. Broke, rearranged his face into a pleasant smile, and said, "Very efficient."

"Thank you, sir."

Turning on his heel, he plunged back into the mass of officers and became indistinct again, a blade of grass among a dozen identical blades. A few of them attempted to catch Taya's eye as they filed out, nodding at her with relief or approbation, *Thank the gods, well done, we didn't want to see another suffocation like last time*, but it did not matter that some of them wanted to distinguish themselves; it did not matter that they weren't all the same. Too many of them had looked up at the gallows with nothing but hunger in their eyes. They had not even seen Death moving in the crowd, swathed in her disguise of rags. They had not seen Love behind her, dressed in his dove-grey suit. He did not often attend these things.

At the very least, though, some chains of—if not honor—at least what they probably thought was *taste* or *decency* prevented Gerhach from publicly retaliating against a child for spoiling his feast. Perhaps he would return to the house later for some private revenge; or perhaps he would pretend it didn't happen. But Taya had counted on him doing nothing with so many witnesses—had gambled everything on it. They weren't like that; they would consider it *untraditional*. And the others served tradition far more than he did. There was nothing they would consider appropriate to do for a hanging that had gone off, after all, precisely to specifications.

Taya felt faint, all the same, as if she had run a long way, even though all she had done was climb the steps up and then down. Gray dots swirled in front of her eyes as the last of the crowd left, and ordinary daylight returned. Anger still remained in the air like smoke; she breathed it in, resigned, knowing she had set the fire herself and could blame no one else if she choked on it now. It came toward her, dressed in its execution-day best.

Hands at her shoulders. "Get her to the carriage. I told you that you should have eaten something. Didn't I tell her?"

"You did, Las."

"I did tell you. I said so. But you never listen to me."

A courier came with Taya's payment two days later, clipped to the death certificate and a copy of the charges, as usual. It was more money than she'd ever seen in her life—a riot of tumbling zeroes across the bank draft like acrobats, above the dead black tree of Gerhach's signature. Aunty Lasidu took Taya and Vil downtown to deposit it, then to the Copper Willow for a sit-down meal, the best one could still have in wartime, in her opinion (this meant, as Taya had deduced, that they served good Treotan food, nothing foreign).

Their table was laid with thick green velvet, a white tablecloth on top of that, and white napkins embroidered with leaves and stems; the air was warm and carried the friendly smell of frying onions. Vil stared around herself as if she had been transported suddenly to another country, instead of the lobby of a hotel barely ten blocks from their own house.

"That was a terrible risk you took," Aunty Lasidu said quietly as they waited for their tea to be brought. "You could have brought ruin down on all of us. All of us. Not just yourself. You disobeyed me, you disobeyed your grandfather, you disobeyed Colonel Gerhach."

Taya nodded.

"And yet." Aunty Lasidu paused as the waiter placed the pot, the teacups, the creamer, the sugar bowl, and the spoons in their places. "I saw no changes in the build."

"I didn't change the build."

"What, then?"

"The trap-door," Taya said, and reached for the pencil in her coat pocket; Aunty Lasidu stopped her. This was not a place where you could write on the napkins. Taya said, "I filled the hollows of the femurs with lead. I bought it on the way back from visiting Grandfather at the orchard. I timed the opening to make sure it hit the man's heels as he fell, so multiplying the extra weight by the—"

"I know my calculations, thank you, Tayavic." Aunty Lasidu's voice remained steely. "Pour the tea."

"Yes'm."

They drank in silence; Taya did not think she could eat, her stomach was twisting so with anxiety, but her aunt insisted, and she ordered chicken soup with fieldcress toast, and pumpkin soup for Vil.

"Grandfather said..."

"Your grandfather who you ignored," Aunty Lasidu said. "Go on."

Taya took a deep breath. "Grandfather has this idea that...that empires move in cycles. That we are in one now, and that everyone is, always. And that cycles must be allowed to continue, because the alternative to that constant motion is that the wheel...*falls*. A flat wheel, he says, prevents progress, causes stagnation, chaos, decadence, rot, as everything backs up behind it. He said the most important thing is that the cycle goes on. That the wheel turns. That we, our family, our people, who were taken over, must ensure it keeps turning."

Aunty Lasidu stirred her tea.

Taya said, "I don't think that's true. Neither do you, I think. Do you? That our only...goal in life should be to keep it rolling for *them?* That we can do nothing for ourselves?"

"No. I don't believe it." Aunty Lasidu sat back, almost smiling; her face remained tense, but there was also a sense of relief, Taya thought, that it had been said out loud. "Tayavic, sometimes you must do something for yourself. That is very true. We teach our children, particularly our girls, that they must live to serve masters. We also teach them that those masters cannot be chosen. But you chose differently, this time. And...you should do it again, *if* you get a chance. Who knows what will happen in the future. Who knows if they will ask you to do it again."

"Do you really think I did the right thing?" Taya felt her eyes fill unexpectedly with tears, and picked up her teacup for something to hold. "It didn't make a difference. The man still died. I made an enemy of Gerhach..."

"Yes. But I think his ego will not let him carry out a vendetta against you. He thinks you are below him; if he had, say, seduced and married you, then you might be raised to his level and he would be able to overlook your origins. But now? He will tell himself he never thought that. He will tell himself you are a nothing, he never considered it, he was only being charitable—giving an apprentice a chance for a prestigious commission. He will disappear from you because he wants to believe himself so far above you. You'll see."

"And you and Uncle—"

"Are we still angry at you?" Aunty Lasidu shrugged. "It will pass. Don't think about it. We are not the masters you serve, Taya. Drink your tea. And make sure Vil eats."

DESIGN CONSIDERATIONS

The goal for every gallows should be to minimize the suffering of the victim, even when counter-indicated by the commission document. This section will outline suggestions for specific mechanisms that may be used for more efficient operation. Knots and rope selection are covered in a later section and will only be referenced here as needed. Refer to the diagram below for a merciful death.

FORSAKING ALL OTHERS

He awoke into a night with no stars, and wondered if he had been killed in his sleep. This was where you went, wasn't it? This place exactly: dark and cold. But there must be flames to torment the deserving so somewhere there must be a red glow, heat, there must be the sound of screams to follow. He rolled over painfully, protecting his eyes from the thornbush under which he had taken refuge, and got up, and patted himself down with frost-stiffened hands: shirt, jacket, satchel. No torture and no light. He was alive.

His name was Rostyn. When he had deserted from his unit he knew this would be the name on every reward poster, so he had chosen a variety of other names for the road, names that fit better with the region through which he traveled. When he had returned to the province of his birth he might adopt Rostyn again, he thought; it was as common as sparrows there. Rostyn, Rosten, Rosteen, Rostin, Rostean, and none of them particularly related (and several with blood vendettas caused by long memories and bad spelling).

Tonight, as with every night for the past three weeks, all he carried was his satchel and his name. He had nothing else. As opportunity arose, he had divested himself of everything that marked him as a soldier—even though this near the front, civilians had appropriated all sorts of discarded or looted military gear for their own use. Earlier in the week he was sure he had seen a prolapsed nanny goat being held together (surprisingly well) with two standard-issue officer-class dress uniform belts.

His eyes had adjusted enough to manage with the sliver of moon now rising over the hills; he clambered out of the ditch, regained the road—a rutted cart-track, hazardous to ankles of any species—and began to walk.

He wanted to run. The military police that pursued him would run if they caught his trail. They could run all night. Sometimes Rostyn wondered whether it had always been so. Always *these particular* men itching to chase after people like him, and never given a paid, socially-approved opportunity until now, until this war and the bounties offered for this quarry. People like him. Peasants in uniform, fodder for the enemy.

Near dawn he left the road, stumbling and nearly collapsing; only the sun warming his back drove him back up, vampire-like, seeking shade and concealment. The fields here were enormous and seemed neverending, but everything ended. He just had to...turn away from the road...turn, make his legs move...

"*Hey.* Get up. They'll find both of us here."

Rostyn rolled over, realizing as he did so that he had blacked out at some point and this was the aftermath: a mouth full of dirt, half-in and half-out of the ditch. He had gone perhaps ten steps past his last urgent thought to turn away from the road. And someone was speaking to him, someone who sounded like home. He let the man pull him to his feet.

"I thought you were dead at first," the other man said, still holding Rostyn's wrist. "When did you leave your unit? Must have been a while."

"I don't know what you're talking about." The denial was automatic, instantaneous. Rostyn pulled his hand back. "I'm not a soldier. Just a man on the road, looking for work."

The man snorted. He looked a little older than Rostyn, perhaps in his midthirties, and along with his accent he had the look of his homeland—wiry, tanned, curling hair between blonde and brown beginning to thin already at browbone and temple. Like Rostyn he wore the hard-wearing homespun of a farmer, and nothing from the army.

"Name's Kalek. Formerly Lieutenant Kalek of the 341st. I know a fellow soldier when I see one, so don't give me that bullshit. I'm not going to turn you in. And you're not going to turn me in. Right?"

Rostyn stared at him. "Right," he said slowly. For a moment he considered whether this might be a ploy by some particularly dastardly branch of military intelligence, sending out so-called fellow deserters to gain the trust of, and then betray, real deserters; then he dismissed it. The MPs were one thing. Intelligence could not waste its time or money on nobodies like him. "Rostyn. 212th. Formerly." He seemed to have trouble forming the words.

"Here. You're about to drop." Kalek led him along the ditch till they found a dried-out gully big enough for them to both sit, then handed Rostyn a leather bottle of water and a few pieces of bread and dried apple. "There's real food back at the house."

"The house?"

Everybody around here calls me Nana. Even those I'm not related to. I don't mind; you get to a certain point and what are you supposed to do about it? Tell them to call me Zelsa instead? Everybody who knew my real name is dead. Including my personal devil—yes, it's a fact, don't argue with me. Our land is the land where they originate, and we all have one. Waiting for us somewhere, endlessly patient—*endlessly*, waiting forever if they need to, so that one day they can meet you. Always with the desire to tempt, betray, bargain, and harm. Not anyone else. Only the one they are waiting for. Almost like love. And it's those as feel unloved as make the quickest victims. All those strange stories you've heard about folks dying young in strange accidents, doing things they'd never do? That's where those stories come from.

Listen. I was born in Ixos, next valley over. We had one ox, ten-twelve chickens, most years about thirty sheep. You can live off thirty sheep but let me tell you, you're still not going to be sleeping on feather-beds or buying shoes for all the kids. As soon as the frost is gone you're out there plowing. All weathers, as soon as you can walk, you're out there beating the bounds, picking odds and ends for the pot, pitching stones at the stray dogs... A boring, miserable life, made just bearable by the knowledge that everybody lived like that, all of us, everybody.

I was about fifteen when the Ustukin invaded, or so they told us. Did they really invade us? Goodness only knows. We found out, oh, six or eight months later... My oldest brother, he ran away to join the army that day, and we got back the box with his ashes, or somebody's ashes, the following Solidarity Day.

Then a few weeks later a shell hit the temple on St. Ratafe's Day. You don't expect foreigners to know our holy days—well, maybe they did, who knows. The way everyone talked about it they sounded like akke-bears in uniform, *hardly* intelligent or malevolent enough to target full temples in tiny villages, more like a hungry antwolf clawing into a nest. What does it care about the ants? But who do you believe?

Anyway. My mother and father died. All my mother's sisters died. I don't need to go on—about half of Ixos died. I was out with a few of my uncles trying to track down some of their sheep that got loose. See the explosion? We felt it in our *teeth*. My uncle would swear later that two of the ewes simply died of fright.

We ran back, we tried to dig people out. Everything was still burning. The ground was burning—I had never seen that before. Deep, deep down, ten or twelve feet down in the pit, it was still red as a bread oven. Like the Palace of Justice after you die. And you know what I asked myself? Little brat as I was? I asked myself whether these...primitive, savage barbarians they told us were invading our country could build and fire a weapon that did that. Or was it perhaps the civilized ones...the ones with scientists in the cities, with fire-flowers at New Year's...

Shells don't come with tickets like the soldiers, at any rate. So I never found out who fired it. But some seeds take a long time to grow. Some seeds you plant and you have to put them out of your mind to go on.

"That's where you're going? Suvelos? You've got people there?"

Rostyn shrugged. Kalek's questions were perfectly innocuous, and you had to fill the hours out here somehow; they were the questions he'd be asking the other man if they had been, say, trapped in a tavern waiting for a storm to pass. "I don't think so," he said after a minute. "I thought it'd be enough to...blend. Thought maybe it'd be the one place no one would turn me in."

"That's true. Hey!" Kalek whistled to one of the ewes that looked about ready to make a break for the weak spot in the fence between the rocks; when she turned her head, Rostyn moved to cut her off. She wandered off, rejoining the others.

Rostyn put a couple more rocks in front of the fence to make it look less alluring, and walked back down to rejoin Kalek.

"But it's also the one place the dogs will come look first," Kalek said, leaning on his crook. He meant the MPs; certainly he rarely referred to anything by its real name, as if someone were always listening to him. "You know, the brass says that's where all the dissidents and agitators come from—that's the center of it."

"Suvelos? I should hardly think so. I grew up there. It's just farmers and farmers' wives as far as the eye can see."

"Well, I grew up there too, and that's what they say."

Rostyn hesitated, thinking. Kalek said he had deserted months ago, and had been slowly working his way west, offering his services to harried farmers to watch, shear, dip, or birth flocks and herds of various beasts for a few pennies a day. Now he had taken Rostyn under his wing, and they split the fee; farmers often preferred two men to one, he had said, and it was true that they were finding work more steadily now. Together they worked all day and ate scraps, but at night they were allowed to sleep in the barns or shepherd huts, and often even the house, if there was an attic or cellar with nothing to steal. It was a living, but it was slow progress.

"I don't have anywhere else to go," Rostyn said. "My list only had one name on it. Where were you thinking?"

"Same place. It was my best idea too."

"Do you have people waiting for you?"

"No. Reason I joined up before the butchers came to feel us up for slaughter. Nothing to lose, no one to threaten."

Rostyn climbed onto the flat stone they'd been using as table and chair for the week and put his crook across his knees. All around the landscape soared and plummeted, like a dropped handful of knives. Grey stone crowned with snow—it wouldn't melt till the end of the summer—and between each peak another little valley just flat enough to plow, another village whose lights, at night, you could cover with the outstretched tip of your thumb. The burned scars of earlier wars had never regrown—still lurked and sulked, black smudges. The MPs would have a hard time here, driving their dogs up and down these slopes. The sheep didn't mind; they were bred to it and produced stunningly good meat and wool from the grass they cropped off the vertical planes of stone.

It was the one place in the entire country where, probably, a man on foot could outpace one on horseback.

But was it better to flee, or disappear? It was not that he expected the people of his homeland to protect him, necessarily, or go out of their way to hide him; but he hoped they would let him be like the little barn lizards, changing color and sitting still as the hawks flew past.

"It could be a waypoint," Kalek said. "If that's what you wanted. Pause there a little, regroup. Then head for the coast—find something on a ship. They don't ask questions there. Don't care about your past."

"They'll be watching the docks. Everybody knows ships hire deserters." Rostyn chuckled weakly, remembering his boyhood and a beating earned for ruining a particular, borrowed jacket. "And I get seasick anyway. They'll throw me overboard not five minutes out."

Kalek smiled. "Then Suvelos it is, I suppose."

―――――――――

After that I moved in with my uncle and his new wife, the Lady Jolilai—this was a joke with the few of us who knew my uncle, if you don't know. Because he was one of those men who could not function long without a wife, and there were none to be had in Ixos, and he went to the city—back then that was called Gahnim, not Whatever-it-is-polis as they call it now—and he went into one of the pleasure-houses and found a woman about his age, and took her home. That was what the owner called all of them, you see. Lady So-and-so, Lady Such-and-such.

The Lady Jolilai—Aunty Joli—was who helped pick out that first husband, and I was grateful for it. My uncle was a nice man, but a know-nothing. You know the type. She snapped up the boy at the fair in the next valley over, talked to his family, bargained the bride-price, and it was all done in about two days.

Did I *mind?* What kind of question is that? Spirits above, spirits below, what a question. I was seventeen, he was seventeen—back then it was considered good luck if your birthdays were close together—and all of a sudden we had our own little house on his father's property, we had our own sheep, our own chickens. I had my own house to run. I had...freedom, of a sort. I woke up in the mornings delirious with it, like a fever. I could do anything I wanted to do. I could put the cups in the cupboard anywhere I wanted to, and they belonged to me. I could keep my egg-money, I could choose the sheep we bought at the exchange. So what if there was a boy in the bed? I could put up with that.

We hadn't been expecting to fall in love, you know, and we didn't. But we became good friends, and I had our first baby two years later—an easy birth, four or five hours, I am telling you the spirits' own truth. A beautiful, healthy girl, fat and kicking. The midwife arrived just in time to catch her and then wouldn't take any fee, but we gave her a big seed-cake anyway—forced it on her. My first husband, he was a good baker.

Death I met with the second baby—she came a couple of hours into the pains and I knew. Many people on my side can see her, you know. And she has ways of making herself seen when she wishes. I hadn't been too worried yet, I thought it would be like the first time, and I said, "Is it me or is it the child?" and she shook her head and settled into the corner to wait, putting her finger to her lips.

I asked her again, as the night drew on. As my husband went for the midwife, and then the midwife borrowed our neighbor's horse and ran for the doctor— Dr. Azim, who still lived in Ixos. And eight hours later he came with Aunty Joli and so there were quite a few folks in the house when both I and the baby died.

Yes, go on and blink. Go on. I don't care. Addled old woman, you think. No. I remember everything.

My husband said later that I had died for as much as, he thought, two or three minutes...the midwife was blowing in my mouth and hammering on my chest with a brick wrapped in a blanket, and Dr. Azim was down at the bottom doing whatever he was doing, and the whole floor, he said, had an inch of blood on it. Then I came back to life. And the baby died.

Azim stepped aside. Death picked up the little body—a boy—and put him on her hip, smearing her beautiful gown with blood, and she walked out into the snowstorm so graceful, just like that, as if it were a clear summer's day, vanishing into flakes so thick you couldn't see your hand in front of your face. I remember the smell of her, not like perfume, but like the clearing up the mountains. Wild blueberries, pine needles, smoke and wet grass. I thought a grand lady like that would wear perfume.

The Treotan came for my husband when our third child—the second who lived—was about four years old, and our eldest daughter was about seven. The draft came for everybody, even us in our little valley. *Had the war truly gone on so long?* we asked. No, there was a treaty signed, that war was over, they said. This was a whole new one.

It was idiotic. It was the games of stupid old men pretending they were playing tsques, moving little marble pieces around on their marble board that cost more than a fast ship. Those pieces were lives, and those lives had names, and one life belonged to me—to *me*, he was *mine*, not theirs—but there were no exceptions even for men who had children. He actually didn't even make it to the front. He died in a training accident. Their fault.

To their credit—the one time, *once*, that I will give them any credit—they sent a big man, a general I think, to the valley in person to talk to me. To say that they were sorry. And I believed him, he had a trustworthy face. He grieved all these young men they had killed, he did not want them to die. He would not to my face admit that this new war was even more ridiculous than the last one, but he grieved. He gave me a box with my husband's things, a certificate, and a letter saying I should get so much money per year from the Treasury of Defense...it wasn't much. But at least this time they *tried*.

The money helped, anyway, because this time both the enemy and our side were giving each other no quarter. They blew up the new train tracks—in those days the tracks had only just been laid, you know, the war set our trains back fifty years compared to the rest of the country—in case the enemy tried to commandeer them, and they knocked holes in ships, they requisitioned horses for the army and they took even oxen and sheep from our farms. And if the enemy came too close to the stockades—if it looked like they might swipe so much as a leg of mutton that was not theirs—why, our men would fire the whole thing so they could have nothing.

We also had nothing. We starved. People died. But that didn't matter to them. That was the first time I saw it, saw that it didn't matter, and I thought... We throw around the word *enemy* far too easily. We do. And we let people tell us what it means. When we should decide for ourselves.

I decided that *enemy* meant anyone who was trying to take food from the mouths of my children.

And I acted accordingly.

Rostyn slept fitfully, dreaming of men with shackles and pistols, bludgeons and dogs. They told him deserting was a crime; they told him he had sworn an oath; they said he was their property and they were recovering it. They had trained him, equipped him, fed him, taught him. How could he take all of their goodwill and effort, and abscond with it in the night like a common thief? How could he leave a hole in the line—how could he fail to protect his brother-soldiers?

They were never my brothers, Rostyn tried to say, but they had already tied a rag around his mouth—a curious thing, a headkerchief embroidered with red and blue flowers, green and white chickens. They must have stolen it from a village woman.

They were never my brothers... But he had left friends behind, yes. He had been trying not to think about it. He should have taken them with him, or...no. He had never made a friend close enough to either excuse or join his cowardice. They were ready to die. Not for the state (he thought) and not for each other, even as their trainers had strenuously tried to indoctrinate them to do, but to kill the enemy...to kill the others.

Rostyn had killed others. Many others. Some of the other men kept count; he had not. And then he stopped wanting to kill them, and the fear of being killed reasserted itself. As if it were some quite reasonable, animal instinct that he could no longer reason himself out of feeling.

In the dream the dogs and the men had the same teeth, and came toward him the same way, slinking, heads steady.

"Wake up!"

"Nn?" Rostyn clawed his way out of sleep, smelling Kalek's sour breath near his face through the sweet odor of last year's hay.

"I heard something. We have to go."

Rostyn cocked his head: yes, the crisp jingle of horses outside, the noise of harnesses and leashes. Strange voices, low and urgent, still rising with that military timbre over the muffled, sleepy voices of the old farmer and her wife.

His heart hammered; for a moment his blood seemed to become fire, so hot he half expected the hay around them to ignite. This was the obvious place to search; the barn below them was too open and empty, the house too small. They had, perhaps, seconds.

"The window."

"We can't get the ladder down."

"We'll have to risk it."

They crawled quickly over the bales of hay, leaving behind the blankets the old woman had given them, and silently pushed open the thick wooden shutters. Darkness outside, another overcast night, no moon.

Rostyn landed with a thud; he hoped his grunt of pain sounded enough like the *chuff* of a horse to go unnoticed for a moment at least, because a moment was all they had. Kalek landed next to him and rolled, and then they were up, covered in the dirt and manure of the farmyard, vaulting the stone wall that formed one side of the pigsty, running in unspoken agreement for the stream that ran between this farm and the next.

They must have covered a mile and a half in their bare feet. Rostyn did not feel the stones nor the broken wood. He ran through the cool dark, arms pumping, stomach empty, driven on by fear. "Can you swim?" Kalek gasped next to him.

"A little. It doesn't matter. There's nowhere else."

They found the stream by ear, a shallow and treacherous little rivulet pocked, as they both knew, with the occasional unbelievably deep sinkhole, as happened when the mountain water came down in the spring and got trapped in eddies that ate away the bottom of the streambed. But it was transportation, and it would break their scent trail, and if they could just endure the cold long enough, perhaps the dogs would not be able to pick it up again when they re-emerged.

None of this needed to be said. None of it could be said, as they clambered down the boulders on the bank and stepped into the icy water, both crying out involuntarily at the impact of it—the cold like a physical blow, like one of the terrible striped fish that lived in the bigger rivers and could bite through bone.

Then it was war again, it was back at the front. The cold water seemed full of the enemy: water made syrupy from flakes of ice forming hands, grasping their limbs, yanking them this way and that, so that even as they left the chest-deep water their arms and legs folded into their bodies and they could not swim. The water stole from them, tearing away Kalek's jacket and shirt, shredding Rostyn's trousers. It slapped them into stones, it squeezed them in its fists like a torturer breaking fingers to scry out secret plans.

"Swim! Swim!" Rostyn heard his mouth say it, but his body did not believe him. With a great effort he forced his limbs straight, or as straight as they would go, and began to paddle furiously with the current. "It's the only way to keep your blood moving. Kalek?"

"I'm here." The voice was faint, terrified. And receding, even though Rostyn had not added much speed to that of the water.

"Kalek!"

"Leave me."

Rostyn glanced back, able to see nothing, trying to listen with his ears: the other man wasn't floating toward him, he must have grabbed onto a stone or the rushes that grew in the slack pockets of water.

"You have to swim or you'll die," Rostyn called back, uncaring whether the dogs or the men heard him. "Come on! Let go. Let go, damn you! I'll keep you from drowning. Come on!"

But he could pause no longer, and he turned back to keep swimming, keep moving. It wouldn't be forever, he told himself, and that kept him going a few more strokes. It can't be forever; it will be only a little part of the night, and every minute that passes is another minute we don't have to endure. It takes us another minute toward morning. It can't be forever.

Kalek was catching up to him, spluttering and thrashing; Rostyn reached out, seized the other man's arm, and somehow, a strange beast of not enough limbs, locked together, they swam on.

———

It was my idea to start robbing the supply lines, yes. Risky? Yes. But both sides had more food, better food, by then, than we did. This was the war after that one, when I had had just about enough. And anyway when you are in your fifties and sixties that is when younger folk cannot help but listen to you, so remember that, if you live so long.

It was dangerous, of course. One couldn't target, you know, the trains or the convoys or anything like that in daylight. But at night, it wasn't so hard to wait till they either stopped to rest—you could get inside their guards fairly easily—or tried to keep going, everybody nodding off. If you want to know the truth, there were three or four times we got in and out without anyone actually noticing. Of course, they don't put the good stuff at the back of the convoy. But there was always something useful, and if you didn't get food, you got something you could trade or sell.

Once there was a shootout, and we got the whole convoy—fifteen carts, and would you believe it, *all* of them full of salt. Bags and bags and bags and bags of salt. We lost two men that night and I kept thinking... We traded your lives for salt. I have to go back, tell your children that Nana lost your fathers, but we have this, see, like white gold... I didn't say that, of course. The men knew what they signed up for. They volunteered.

We'd come back and Dr. Azim would dig out the bullets and patch up the saber-cuts, and out we'd go again. After that it was just a step or two to running guns to the insurgents, you know how it goes. They're young boys, usually too young for the draft, led by a couple of walking dead even older than me—fellows who maybe survived one or two of the wars before they aged out of conscription, and learned their tactics from a book. We didn't start with the guns, of course. Just ammunition. Then grenades, *then* the guns. And carts and horses too if we could get them. Mountains up here are good for that.

It was one of those nights that I saw Death for the second time, you know. We had struck a horse-train—of course, they don't do those any more, you're confused. One cart to house the guards and grooms, and then a long line of about thirty horses, replacements for the cavalry losses. We wanted those horses. The Avalaians had good horses for the mountains, short fellows with strong legs, not like the stringy spidery ones they keep breeding in our cities. You don't want a racehorse on a farm. You want a warhorse. Anyway, it was an ambush; the horses were bait, and we fell for it like a bunch of ninnies.

They shot me right here—a really lucky shot, one in a million chance. Missed my liver by about the width of the bullet. Wrecked up this, that, and the other inside me, but if you get shot in the liver, I don't need to tell you, you're a goner. And I fell and there she was, Death, kneeling next to someone else—one of the guards, I think, staying beside him with her hand on his forehead till he stopped moving. And then she came over to me.

I told her hello, and complimented her gown; and she said, "Thank you. I had it specially made for the occasion."

"The occasion of my death?" I asked her.

"No," she said. "A greater death than yours... You will not see it coming over the horizon, Zelsa." She was right, too. We found out a few days later—or in my case, about two weeks later, because I was abed—that the night we had gone for the horse-train was the last night of the war. The armistice was signed the following morning at dawn. We did not see it coming over the horizon.

That was the end of that, I thought. No more war, no more resistance. No need to do anything but putter around the house with my third husband—he died about five years ago—and look after the chickens and the grandkids and knit. And we had quiet. We had a little quiet.

But there is something inside the men who run this place that can never rest, and must always fight, always hungry for power...something sick, hot and stinking as gangrene...as if they had all eagerly signed the deal with those we warn our young ones about, as if they hadn't listened to us at all. I suppose we'll never know.

"Is that it?"

"I think so." Rostyn swayed, overcome with vertigo, and sat down; this happened a few times a day now to both of them, and Kalek sat next to him without a word of comment. It would pass soon.

It did look like his old village—then again, all the villages they had seen as they had crept up and down the mountains, not daring to use the old passes, had looked like this. Each diaspora was composed of people who had a perfectly good idea of what a house, a farm, and a village should look like, and they all adhered relatively closely to that ancestral vision even in places so isolated that they no longer had a common tongue with the adjacent valley.

Stone cottages to keep in the warmth in the winter, slate roofs to shed the snow and the rain, terraced fields so you didn't go arse over teakettle with the plow every time. Flowers and ferns painted on the white wood shutters, no two the same. It was quite a bit bigger than he remembered, and that surprised him; he had expected that after moving to the city, and then training in the army, he would have found the place diminished, proportionally smaller to the eyes of an adult than to the eyes of the boy he had been.

"What's all that?"

"What?" Rostyn shielded his eyes, frowning. There was some commotion down there, certainly—a procession of people marching down the main street, heading from the bigger stone building that he vaguely remembered as the council house to a sprawling house on the outskirts of the village, near a perilous but carefully fenced-off cliff of bare blue stone. "I think that's my grandmother's old house."

"Really?"

"Yes, she added rooms to it five or six times over the years... She never measured or anything, just dug up the turf and got people to help her stack rocks. That's why it looks so strange. She took people in. Not just us kids. Whoever came around."

"What are they yelling?"

"Can't hear. Come on." He glanced back to Kalek, who hadn't moved; the man's face was creased with hesitation only, not fear. Rostyn said again, "Come *on*. Maybe they won't hide us, maybe they'll drive us out. But first they'll feed us and give us clothes and boots. It's one of those honor things. I promise."

"All right."

———

What I should have done, really, was get a better look at them as was waiting at the blacksmith's; you know how it is. You look at a crowd and you think you know every face in it. Well, that's your memory filling in for your eyeballs. There were strangers there, and it was one of them that went out screaming and upset the whole apple-cart. So-called "military police," bunch of rats in uniform. And them that dragged me in, a little old lady like me—that's how I tried to play it, anyway. All the witnesses were village folk and swore to it, too. Didn't help at first. What did help was when the body—no, let me go back, I missed the first part.

It was my heart and I always knew it was going to be my heart. And when it started up—the noises in there, the clanging and banging like a broken bell, and I started to go to the floor—I looked for her again, I thought I'd see her head rising above the heads of the others, thought I'd see her expensive shoes on the floor, hear them in the gravel. But I didn't. And there was dear old Dr. Azim all of a sudden, pushing his way in, "Let me through! Let me through! Everyone out!" and the kiddies, even the big growed-up men shouting "Nana!" like I'd forgotten who I was just because my heart wasn't beating right...quite a commotion for a minute. Darkness coming down soft, like a blanket.

And then he was next to me, and whispering, "I can fix it—certainly I can fix it—no heart is as broken as you think. But just this once, and never again, I will ask for payment..."

"Just this once," I said, because his face was so close to mine—I could see all the silver in his whiskers, no different from the day we met when I was a girl. And I said to him, I said, "I've knowed it was you for seventy-odd years, you old bastard. You never fooled me for as much as one minute. All I needed was for you to show your hand."

"I beg your pardon," he said, and my heart gave one almighty thump and I reached up—well, you have to, don't you? Once you know who it is, once your personal devil takes his mask off. It was a hammer I got, one of those big lump hammers, and it turns out you don't need to hit someone too hard with that to kill 'em.

I got up, I dusted off my dress, and explained that he'd finally revealed himself—and then those strangers in the back, the ones in uniform, started up a howl and commotion like you never heard. Down we went to where they'd set up in the council house, and in I went to the cells in the back—you know the ones, the little drunk tank they usually have to spend an hour finding the locks for the doors.

Rostyn stared at her, mouth hanging half-open.

"More tea?" she said brightly.

"No...Nana, I...I didn't know *any* of this. My parents never said...I never saw...and you *killed* a man? *Yesterday?*"

"Suit yourself." She poured for herself and topped up Kalek's cup. Her hands shook now, and she had lost weight—too much, Rostyn thought—but she was still the snapping, hawklike woman he remembered from his youth, white-haired and quick-moving under the voluminous fabric of her peasant coveralls. "And no, Bonny, I didn't kill a man. I killed a devil. Which is what I was gettin' to—they'd taken the body, you see, for evidence, and even the fancy fellow with all the brass on his chest had to admit he was stumped when the body started spouting green smoke and curling up on itself." She sipped her tea. "Like a bug in a fire."

"What?"

"It takes a while," she clarified. "I s'pose the devils would control it if they could, but for a while they seem like normal bodies, and then their true nature returns, as it always does. Now, in the old days, they'd turn that around, see, and accuse whoever killed the devil of being a witch—say that *they* were the ones making the smoke and causing the flesh to twist up and change like that. And a fair few innocent folks were killed for it. But can you see an officer of the Treotan army doing it? He couldn't either." She chuckled. "So he didn't. Sent me home on 'house arrest' while they figure out what to do, and that's when I came to my front door and saw you two creatures lying in front of it like sick cats."

"N...Nana," Kalek ventured. "You're saying the military police are here though? Here, right now? In the village?"

"Yep. Got here a few days ago. Wasn't sure what they were waiting for." She raised what was left of her eyebrows at them. "Now I'm sure."

"We'll go," Rostyn said at once, half rising in his chair. "We're putting everyone in danger, they'll arrest you for harboring fugitives—we'll keep heading west, we'll go to—"

"Nonsense," she said. "Not on my watch. I'd as soon let them catch you as I would let them find the knife I have pinned in my drawers."

"*Na*na. Still?"

She put them in a cellar accessed not through a trap-door, as were the other cellars in the house, but through a door in the wall, down a narrow stone staircase just wide enough to fit if they both walked sideways instead of forward.

The room was surprisingly comfortable—a few coin-sized gaps in the stone allowed some air, though of course it was still stagnant and stuffy, smelling of wet earth, and there were cots, tables, chairs, an oil lamp, and a couple of grimy decks of cards and some moisture-swollen books.

Kalek lit the lamp and held it close to the topmost cover. "*Butterflies and Lovebirds: A Knightly Romance.*"

"I've read that one. What else is there?"

"Shh!"

Voices above them, the tramp of boots. Rostyn and Kalek froze; after a few seconds, with great presence of mind, Kalek snuffed the lamp. Earth and bits of rust and lichen rained down into their upturned faces, but they could not stop staring, as if they could see through the floor the men who had arrived so quickly after they had been spirited away. What were they saying? This was the obvious place to come—this place was the center of the anti-war movement, certainly the old lady wasn't *part* of anything but she knew things, old women always did, maybe she hadn't seen anything but someone must have said something, they had to ask her some questions...

Rostyn gritted his teeth, wild with frustration and helplessness. He had done this, brought all this down upon the village. And all because he could not die like they wanted him to, die in the service of the state... What had Nana said, as she was making the tea? *Maybe it's time for the enemy to win once and for all. Trounce them properly, and then they'll stop bullying everybody else for good...* He could see the sense in that now. A coalition of nations needed to come together against the empire. Just once, as she said. And tell them to knock it off.

But it did him no good, it did his cowardice no good, his conscience no good, to think grand things about governments and treaties while he was down here in the mold-smelling dark with a coward just like himself. The voices drew closer, retreated, approached again. It sounded as if one of the men was leaning against the wall that concealed the staircase, just five or six feet above their heads.

And then his grandmother was shouting, real anger in her thin, piercing voice: "You have no right! Yes, you! You have no right to be here—and you'd better get out, or by the spirits—don't you touch me, you bitch's bastard!"

It only took a single *thud* against the wall and Rostyn could not take it any more, was pushing Kalek behind him as he ran back up the stairs, fumbled with the bolt, put his shoulder to the secret door, and attempted to run into the kitchen—tripping heavily, first, and catching himself on his hands and knees, over the prone and moaning body of a fully-uniformed sergeant.

"Nana!"

The officer holding the old woman's wrist turned to stare at him as she continued to writhe and fight him, snakelike but too small to make a difference in his grip. Rostyn charged him, sending all three of them to the floor.

The man fought as Rostyn had been trained to fight, as someone trained to believe unquestioningly that retreat was shameful, peace was shameful, negotiation and surrender were shameful. Rostyn, meanwhile, fought as if he had four older brothers and no mere training could hope to scrub away the dirtiness of their technique. The final blow was Rostyn's bony knee meeting the other man's jaw with a terrible crunch, sending two teeth flying.

Kalek joined the fight, and for perhaps a full minute—fights always seemed longer in books than they were in real life—they struggled and grunted with the remaining three officers without comment, ignoring their shouts to stop, *Stop it, this is treason, stop, lie down, put your hands on your heads.*

At last Kalek regained his feet, panting, and pulled Rostyn up. Kalek had taken the men's small service pistols, which in the melee they had not had time to remove from their buttoned holsters, and had dropped all of them into the potato bag except for the two he had kept.

Rostyn held a hand out for one; and Kalek looked at him, calm, blood trickling from the cut above his eye that seemed to be his only wound, and said, "No. I'm sorry."

"Sorry for what?"

Kalek nudged one of the prone officers, who got up slowly, dusting down his sharp black uniform. Rostyn realized with a sick, cold, familiar sensation—yes, like that first step into the mountain stream—that the man had been shamming, and Kalek had not fought him at all. And it had all gone unnoticed in the scrum, and now...now...

Rostyn backed up a step, and gently pulled his grandmother to her feet, leaning her against the wooden counter that held the basin and pitcher for washing dishes. "All right," he said. "All right, only leave Nana out of it. Can you?"

Kalek shook his head, still training one gun on the officer and one on Rostyn. "Sorry, can't do that either."

He jerked his chin at the officer, a handsome bewildered young man with straight fawn-brown hair and dark eyes. "You there. Lieutenant."

"Vessough."

"Yes, whatever. This is the deserter you were sent to find, wasn't it? Bonnaryn Rostyn."

"Yes."

"Well, he's yours now. I'm turning him in. And the old woman will tell you everything about the resistance here, or whatever it's calling itself—the thieves and dissidents and antisocial vermin and suchlike. She's the beating heart of it. Your first mistake was letting her out of prison."

Vessough blinked at him, the doe-like eyes unchanging. His voice was lightly bantering, still filled with disbelief. "And what do you get out of it, my treacherous friend? Having betrayed your fellow deserter, I suppose you would not then betray the Treotan army to the enemy later on? Calumny is a hard habit to break, once it's begun."

"No. All I want's amnesty. A promise I'll get away clean and no dogs will come after me. Simple as that." His face twisted. "They're yours, man! I'm giving them to you! Take them!"

Rostyn felt something touch his back—his grandmother, but not her fingers. Slowly he moved one hand behind himself, trying to make no noise. Something smooth...the handle of a knife. Wasn't there a whole series of jokes about bringing a knife to a gunfight? Still, it was something, and supposing he could take down Kalek, it would be well worth getting shot if it spared his grandmother and her network...

Somewhat to his surprise he found that he was still thinking about it, weighing the pros and cons, wondering about the caliber of the bullets (the pistols were beautiful, but much smaller than the handguns issued to infantry), as he launched himself at Kalek with the knife, lunging to one side rather than coming in low, knowing the other man would have expected him to try to knock the gun-holding arms ceilingward.

Both pistols went off—once, twice, finally five times, and then Rostyn was rising, gasping, his vision constricted to a pinprick, all else darkness. Kalek writhed on the floor, the knife moving with him where it was embedded low on his right-hand side. Then he stopped writhing and lay still, and blood spread around him with a slight, alarming noise—a kind of pulsing splash.

"There, see?" His grandmother moved shakily toward him. "What did I tell you about the liver?"

"Are you all right, Nana?"

"It's fine." Four of the shots had gone wild; one had struck her in the upper arm, around which she now clutched a stained kitchen rag, still smelling of onion and garlic.

Vessough, meanwhile, had wisely not made a move toward the fallen guns. "Excuse me," he called as Rostyn fussed over the wound, looking for a bigger cloth to add more pressure. "You've just murdered a fellow soldier, Private Rostyn."

"That one was never in the army," Nana said firmly. "You can check your records for him till the day after the end of time and never find him. He's..."

"What?"

"A devil." Rostyn sighed and added one more knot to the towel he had finally found. "She's about to tell you he's a personal devil. We have them here. The proof is that he betrayed me in the end."

"No it isn't, Bonny," she snapped. "It was his reaction when I was telling the *story* of the devils. Weren't you looking at his face? No, men never do, they're always looking at hands, like they're bracing up for a fight. If he really grew up here like he said he did, he'd have known that story already. Yes, even if he forgot, like you did. Then it would be like a coming home. But he never heard it before in his life. They don't know their own legends; they only do what they're created to do."

"Nana—"

"Aha, here we go."

Rostyn turned, as did Vessough, as half a dozen villagers—four men, two women—politely pushed through the open door and began to bind the fallen officers with rope, hand and foot. "Just you now, fancy-pants," Nana said to Vessough, not without some sympathy. "I suppose you want to get out of here alive, hmm? And all your men?"

"*Yes* ma'am," Vessough said automatically, his face crimsoning.

"Then you'll leave this place, under our terms and like we say, and you'll give your word as an officer and, I suspect, a gentleman—you're some kind of minor nobility, aren't you? Yes, nod nod—that you won't be back. Not for my grandson, not for anybody. You've kicked a hornet's nest here, my lad. Go back and don't tell anybody you did it, and don't let 'em see the stings. Do we have a deal?"

Vessough nodded. "No need to shake on it," he said. "We'll...we'll be well out of your hair. I swear."

"Good."

When they had gone, dragging out the quick and the dead alike, Rostyn sagged into one of the kitchen chairs and exhaled for what felt like the first time all day. The blows he had taken could not but catch up now that the excitement had worn off; his ears were ringing and, he realized, had been ringing for some time. And he still couldn't see properly. That was the altitude and the shock as much as anything, he diagnosed himself. It would wear off soon.

"I'll go," he said. "You can't trust the word of these men, you can't trust anybody. They'll say anything. I'll clear out, and you can..."

"Don't be silly." His grandmother winced, and leaned against the wall, studying him with her bird-bright eyes. "My friends will be back soon, and we'll all need to eat. It's been a long day. Go outside and get one of those brown hens—they don't lay any more and I've been saving 'em. Go on, get. We have to start now or she won't have time to soften up on the fire for supper. I can patch you up once the pot is on."

"Yes, Nana." He got up, paused in the doorway, aware that his boots were sticking in the blood of the dead man. "He...you *really* think Kalek was my personal devil?"

"Doesn't matter. You'll see tomorrow if I was right. And anyway, what's one body more or less at this point? At least this one bought you some peace. What about the other ones?"

"I don't know." He looked outside for a moment: the flowers, the fields, the white specks of sheep on their impossible slopes, the iron-grey stone. A homecoming he did not deserve; a home he was supposed to have received as reward for suffering in the war. A home he had nearly destroyed by coming. He sighed. "What *is* it that you do here now, anyway?"

"I'll tell you while we eat. And before you ask—yes indeed, we can always use another pair of hands."

THE GENERAL'S TURN

So it begins. And the play is conducted upon the gears of a clock.

Constructed inside this ancient cathedral the bright artifice of turning brass was by necessity laid flat to provide a stage; it looks wrong but it all works to keep time. There is a bell, though it does not strike the hours. No electric lights are allowed; we often bring in lanterns, but tonight the cavernous space burns gold and amber from the flaming city. It is bright enough to read a newspaper.

Balanced on the largest gear, the captured criminal looked around, dazed, his khaki uniform a ghostly presence against which his golden-brown hands and face stood out like ink. Around him climbed the ranked gears, twenty-four in all, threaded on axles as thick as the masts of ships. He said, "Where... What is this place? What are you doing?"

"We have not yet begun," I said, stretching luxuriously and putting my hands behind my head. I would have attempted a reassuring smile, but did not; I know what I look like. "You will hear a chime."

The boy stared at us, the dozen spectators in a hundred plush red theatre seats. I thought he probably could not see the faces of the other officers. Only the gilt buttons on their black uniforms, like so many eyes in a forest.

"And then what?"

"And then the players will join you on the stage." I gestured at the darkness behind him, where waiting things gleamed in the reflected firelight from the small, stained-glass windows. "*Players*, such a useful word. I could have said *actors*, but they are not acting; they are playing a game. Tell me your name and unit, please."

"You already know that," he said suspiciously.

"For the sake of these fine gentlemen, who did not have the pleasure of traveling with you from the front. Please."

"P...Private Ensi Stremwynn. Of the 514th." He swallowed visibly, his throat moving like a snake. "The others in my unit..."

"Don't worry about them," I said. "This is a game for one."

There was a man, you know, in the far north of my province. This was what he liked to do (so the papers said): He liked to steal a child, spirit it away to his cottage in the wild forest, where he had built a cellar resembling a dollhouse. Every inch locked up tight, but decorated with ribbons and lace and pretty things. Paintings. Toys. Then he would dress up these children. Rouge them like a doll and demand they play with him. And then, of course, after a few weeks, he would kill them.

And that is how the boy looks now: as if he has been captured by this man. His gaze accuses us of impossible, disgusting depravity.

Nonsense, I want to tell him. *Don't look at me like that. We are not perverts and kidnappers. This is war.*

"Very well. The others have been executed. You don't want to die like them." I yawned. "Do you?"

"I'm not afraid to die!"

"Of course not. But you want to live, naturally."

"Tell me about this *game!*" His voice cracked at last, and behind me someone applauded alone: three or four sarcastic little pats of the hand.

"You have been chosen," I said. "Save your breath, save your voice. You will need it."

"For *what?*"

I met his gaze steadily. Before you die you can eat. And let this be your last meal: beauty. Do not step into the flat-bottomed boat and say to the ferryman: *They starved me, I had nothing for my eyes and heart to eat up before I died, and now I am empty.* You will die full. Filled to the brim. Your whole skull abrim, ribs abrim. "To earn a dignified death. A beautiful, honorable death. Not dying in the seam."

He started, then turned his back on me. Stung that I had guessed.

I know this boy. Boys like this. Born of coal, their forefathers dead at thirty with lungs you could burn to heat a barn. Before the army starved him he was a big sturdy lad, fine fodder for the pit. Now he is barely held together by his uniform, a wrapped packet of bones like you would get from the butcher for your dog.

At any rate, if you are a child of coal you don't fear war as it turns out. You have been born to fight. Fight the darkness, the seam itself, the crumpling shafts, the poison gas, the corrupt foremen, the betrayal or neglect or sacrifice of your fellows. The way the mountain shuts on you like the mouth of one of those great lizards in a book. *Crunch*. They make good soldiers, these miners' boys.

"It is a guessing game," I said. "You will have to guess the identity of one of the players."

"Fuck you, fuck this play." The boy spat, or tried to; his mouth clicked drily. "I don't know any of these people! How could I—"

"They don't know you either. I will tell you who you have to identify though."

"Who?"

"Death." I admit I am hurt, slightly, that he has not heard of my country's grand and ancient ceremony, this signature honor bestowed upon a captured enemy who could have been shot or sabered in a slaughterhouse like a steer. (We like doing mass executions in slaughterhouses; they are very handy in terms of cleanliness, gutters, lighting, and so on.)

His mouth hung open. Waiting to see if I was joking, if the others would laugh. Death, of course, lies like a mist over the land; millions of our countrymen have been killing one another for three years. Everything stinks of it, the water tastes of it. But Death as well as death attends this ceremony when we hold it.

"You have till the clock strikes, Private Stremwynn. Which should be around dawn. If you correctly identify who plays Death, you will be spared. If not, you have the choice of being hanged on the gallows currently being constructed in Old Parade Square, which will be public; or being crushed between the gears here, which only we will witness.

"In either event your remains will be interred with all honor in the Royal Cemetery, and caretakers will plant runnelvines around your grave to preserve your flesh. Hmm?"

Stremwynn looked down at the line of guards, making the predictable calculation. A dozen men stood in the space between the first row of seats and the massive stone block supporting the gears. Armed; the boy saw, I knew, the glint of their sidearms.

"They won't shoot you," I called out. "They'll just put you back on the stage. Come now, Private. Show some backbone. What would General Narolo think if you did yourself in?"

"Let me live," he said. "I'm a prisoner of war, there are *rules*—"

"We don't like other people's rules."

He raised his voice. "I don't ask for mercy. Only fairness."

"Reciprocity is for children and gangsters," I said. "*Oh, oh, he has one more biscuit than me!* Everyone else understands that life is a set of scales."

I didn't invent this ceremony. We've done it for five hundred years. Three dozen wars. The same clock, the gears replaced or sharpened or milled or greased; the same foundation carved from bedrock to support its enormous weight. We carry the ceremony out only when needed. We are not barbarians. We do not do these things at a whim. We happen to think there is something noble about it, and therefore about us. Nobility is the practice of not spitting upon tradition.

And that is why we picked him, and executed the other captured soldiers in a more efficient fashion.

Nobility, too, is inefficient. Famous for it.

Stremwynn swayed, and braced himself on the gear behind him.

"Then let us begin," I said.

"No!"

I paused to enjoy the chuckles of the audience, then nodded to the lieutenant supervising the handful of prisoners winding the clock spring. At his unseen rope-tug a small, sweetly silver tone sounded over their groans and whimpers.

And the players came dancing from the darkness, a score of figures masked, gowned, suited, costumed as animals or fae or fools, and they bowed, wafting a mingled scent of perfumes and colognes, the cedar chips packed with the outfits to keep off moths, and damp young skin.

"Ah," murmured General Cjesev, one row behind me and three seats over. "*Isn't* it just."

"Shush," I said. The master of the ceremony cannot speak to the audience, or vice versa; he should have passed a note. The so-called nobleman and his terrible manners.

The boy froze as the players distributed themselves on the now-turning gears, laughing as they rescued coattails or feathers, the trains of dresses or a protruding ribbon. Their finery was slightly shabby, many outfits having been ripped and torn from careless players.

"You're insane," said Stremwynn, as if it had just occurred to him. He backed against the axle of his gear, curling his hands around the oily brass. "You're all *insane*! They told us you were despots, they didn't say you had all gone *mad*!"

"Is that what they call us? I'm hurt." I'm delighted; I want to give the boy a medal before we kill him. Something nice for the noose to rest against. "Well, never mind," I said soothingly. "Gallows or gears? You can choose at the end if you like."

"You are monsters!" the boy shouted.

"But you are a convicted war criminal," I said. "*You* are the villain here. Not us." Behind me, someone could hold it in no longer and guffawed, and the laughter caught from row to row like the city burning outside. Colonel Mezhi would have started that; I had as much as felt his spittle on my neck. He was a crass boor, a jumped-up thief; I liked him for never hiding what he was. "The game has begun, Stremwynn. Off you go."

"But I... How can I possibly..." The laughter had rattled him, and for a moment he visibly warred between fury and bewilderment. "How can... Death is a process, a...a biological..."

"Time is wasting, Private."

He set his jaw, and walked slowly around the edge of his gear, and stepped up onto the next, and the game began.

I smiled, and dug some sweets out of my pocket. The most wonderful moment of any war! From outside drifted the friendly *tap-tap-tap* of the carpenters at work on the gallows. You had to be careful, building with bone. It was not like wood or metal but more alive than either: prideful, fussy, prone to shattering, bending. In fact when you sat down and thought scientifically about it, bone is a ridiculous choice. But in life it bore weight without complaint or flaw, you could say that much. It did bear weight. And anyway it was the spectacle that mattered: that pink-white geometric perfection against the dawn sky.

As if drugged, or knocked on the head, Stremwynn wobbled over to the gorgeously posed players, who leaned toward him with all their perfume and pageantry as if to not miss a single word. "If I ask you if you are Death, must you answer truthfully?" Ah: good man. Trying to figure out the rules.

"No," replied a tall man in a cat mask and tuxedo, flicking his glossy red wig away from his face. "But you may know from other ways when Death speaks."

Stremwynn clambered upward, bracing himself on brass and stone, shying away from those who fondled his hair, brushed invisible dust from his uniform, offered him flowers or sweets from secret pockets. Wisely, he took none. He vanished in a cloud of satin and velvet, fur and brocade, his hands moving dreamily across silken bare backs, brushing their hair over his scarred young knuckles, stroking the feathery napes of men, touching bare earlobes. I thought he felt for wings or horns. He would not find them.

Behind me the watchers fell silent, as if we were at the ballet. And I had been to the ballet with these men. They chuckled under their breath, made lewd comments about the dancers. But this silence seemed sacred.

And it should be. Show some goddamned respect. They had not attended as many of these as I had, nor presided over any, and they never would: not Mezhi the brutish mobster, not Cjesev the deranged nobleman, who wanted it most. We all felt Death's presence here.

"What are you asking them, Private?" I said. "Are you asking the right questions?"

"Yes," he said. His voice slurred. "No. What do you care?"

Their footsteps pattered across the brass. Laughing, a girl draped all in glitter and string escaped him, and he pursued her, slipped, dangled from the teeth by his fingertips, then dropped with a grunt back to a larger gear.

"Ah, is it her, do you think? Have you chosen so quickly?"

"I'm not saying till the end," he growled. "Because you lie. And they lie. And it doesn't matter, does it? There's no way to win. You just want to laugh at me."

"Oh, well don't play then," I said airily. "If you like, you can just lie down. That's a good gear to lie on, don't you think? Nice and smooth. Lie down and give up. Hmm? The way your army does. The way your fellow-fighters did. None of them resisted, did you know that? They just lifted their heads for the knife." I paused, and studied my nails. "Like dogs looking up at their masters one last time."

He stared at me, this sentient bag of bones with his eyes candleflames in sunken sockets, reflecting on taut dark cheekbones. "No," he said. "I will play. And I will break the rules if I want," he added with a snarl. "You rigged the game, you rigged the war. You do nothing with honor. Not this. Not anything."

"I think you will choose the gallows, at the end," I said. "Because you think we would enjoy watching you scream between the gears. You'd rather have it quiet."

He twitched again with rage, this time falling off his gear and onto the stone. I craned my head sympathetically as he rose shaking, apparently unhurt, dusting himself down.

"You have to die," I said. "That has been determined for you."

"Not if I win."

"No one's ever won," I said regretfully; there *is* a way to win, always has been, but naturally we never speak of it till the end. "Stremwynn, that's a very old name, isn't it? In Avalaia, I mean. Yes, I have made some linguistic study. Your name once meant a ferryman. I rather like that. When you are dead you can go on any of the five rivers, not just the one for warriors. And you can say, *It is me, the ferryman; let me aboard.* Perhaps they'll even employ you. Though I don't know rightly what you would need money for in paradise."

Colonel Mezhi laughed, and a moment later something poked my neck: a folded note scribbled on the back of a cigarette packet. *Tell him*, it said, *he will need to pay for his women, for no one would otherwise fuck him even in paradise.* I laughed, and relayed the message. Stremwynn pretended not to hear it.

"Supposing you do not wish to be buried in the cemetery?" I said. "Then we can put you on the river Rath. I think part of it is not on fire. What do you think? Only, there would be no beautiful grave for your family; we give them a special visa, you know, to visit any time. There may well be a statue. We might commission a poet for the plaque."

"Stop it!" he screamed. "Stop it! Shut up! Shut your filthy mouth! Why did you pick me, you monster? What did I do? Why didn't you pick someone else?"

"Because I am the one allowed to choose." I settled another candy against my back teeth. "Go on. You have only till the bell rings, and you do not know when that will be."

How? Why him? I never knew. We had rounded up the survivors of his unit, thirty-seven men, and I had paced the lineup. The mud on their faces and uniforms was beginning to freeze, sprouting white hairs of ice.

And only his eyes were still on fire while the others were extinguished, not even a wisp of smoke.

I had chosen him because the others fought for duty, and he fought for hatred. Had he learned it on the battlefield? Had *we* infected him with it, this disease of fever and flame? Well, no matter. His eyes held the only light of the day.

And so I marked the traditional streak of black ink across his startled face; and the guards hustled him off to scrub and feed him.

They handcuffed him across from me for our ride back to the capital. A long trip this time, switching tracks when the rails were sabotaged or sunk or blocked by the corpses of trains looted for coal and parts. Slowly we abandoned the churned mud of the front and flew through those places not yet reached by fighting, through the gold-green grass billowing like a silk scarf, through forests bright and hot with spring leaf, and still the boy did not relax.

I removed my jacket, showed him my hands, a posture of perfect vulnerability: *See, I open myself to you, like a book.* I told him stories of my childhood, my village. The bones of huge animals I had studied while attending the university in Rathmenn, whose towers he would see as we pulled into the station.

But despite my encouragement, plying him with wartime luxuries, sweets, cigarettes, good white bread, he spoke only to say his name and division. Which he knew I knew, for I had examined his wallet as he watched, the sad thing squashed thin as an autumn leaf. An identification card, a ration card, a medical card listing on one side which shots he'd gotten and on the other the diseases he might catch from our revolting soldiers. And a single smudgy photograph of three people, two men and a woman, young. Family? Friends? Lovers?

Ştremwynn looked away when I held it up and translated aloud the inscription: a date four years ago, and *The old house in Tanad, before the accident.*

He was twenty years old.

The brass teeth flickered and danced in the firelight; the players, leaping lightly from gear to gear to elude Stremwynn, began to sweat. Their skin became gilded, their strong young bodies like statues. The boy himself still staggered as he walked, his boots loud and graceless. "The entire world will descend on you when they hear about this. They'll lock you in an asylum. And they'll feed you charcoal and hold your head under ice water, trying to fix your brains."

"Oh, how tedious," murmured Cjesev. "How's one supposed to enjoy oneself."

"Yes, it's worse than eating popcorn at the opera," I murmured back. He sat back, vindicated, sulking. "You're talking to the wrong people," I said to Stremwynn. "Go on, talk to them. Not us."

"Why? They're lying. They lie like you lie. Death isn't here."

"We're not lying," I said. "No part of this ceremony is a lie."

"Then it is the only thing you haven't lied about for five hundred years. And I'll tell you something else, monster," he added, swiveling suddenly with his eyes shining again.

My stomach sank, and I wrestled not with fear but with confusion: What did I have to fear from him? But no, I have seen too many faces in my time. I know faces too well. It is my curse: because no one looks that way unless they are burdened with a secret like a spear, meant to be hurled to kill.

"I'll tell you something else. And Narolo can't court-martial me for this, because I'll be dead. I suppose he could spit on my grave. But you smell that smoke? Hear those screams? That wasn't us. We haven't dropped so much as a firecracker on you in two weeks. That's you, that's all on you. I bet you even gave the order, Vessough. You people bombed your own capital because you thought one of our divisions had gotten over the wall and hid in the warehouse district...we never did. We lied. Fed garbage to your spies. Didn't you know that? Didn't you know you weren't the only ones who could lie? And you bombed your babies and your old women. How do you like that? Rig the fucking game!"

Stremwynn laughed, clutching his sides theatrically; the players scattered around him like startled birds. I did not laugh. Behind me, in the velvet seats, rose a velvet hush. I waited for Mezhi's coarse guffaws to begin, but heard only the tick and clonk of the gears, the boy's hysterical, forced cawing.

Could it be true? He was right in one respect: I'd heard of the order, though I had not approved it as the capital was not my jurisdiction. How could he have known that, having come into the city last night?

And the answer was: They knew, they all knew. His entire doomed division. Perhaps Avalaia's whole army. They had seen our tactics and thought: *So, they think they are the only ones with a thumb on the scales.*

"Now I know you are truly unafraid to die," I said lightly, though it strained my face and throat with the effort. "Supposing you win the game and return to your side? They'll hang you themselves."

"Fuck you."

"And you'll never see the old house in Tanad again."

He turned back toward me, and lifted his cap, stroked his sleeve across his forehead, replaced the cap. "Supposing I win the game," he said quietly, over the rustles of the other officers as they leaned forward impatiently to hear. "Supposing I do? I will not leave this place. I will kill you with my bare hands."

"For this?"

"For everything."

For everything, I thought, unable to stop myself. For the one thing that we cannot take back. For the lives taken in this war. Not for his own.

Yes, we are cruel. Yes, the world does not use that word as a compliment the way we do. Yes, the world will learn of this and they will see what we call nobility, honor, tradition, and they will call it sickness.

Very well.

The dead cannot return. Not by my hand, not by his. I am tired, I am older than I look. Probably this will be my last ceremony. But I have never prevented a death. No, not a one. Not a single one. I have never saved a life.

Supposing we both played for that? Against Death, against the watchers, against the players. Supposing I put a single extra piece on his side of the board.

There are no rules against it, are there? No, they will not be able to cite a single one.

For the main way the game is rigged, of course, is that there is a moment—about ten seconds—in which all the gears line up, once and never again, in a perfectly straight staircase leading to a hidden door tucked into the place where ceiling and wall meet. The stairs cannot be seen until that moment, and that is when the players are coached to do their utmost both to distract and to hide the fact that they are distracting the player, so that he does not spot it.

No one ever has. That is how cunning the alignment is.

But how, how? The others could not know. I was growing excited and made myself remain still, pasted an expression of light distaste upon my face. What was this? Proximity to life instead of death? No, Death was still here, and death too. Breathing on me with its cool, soil-scented breath.

But life too smells of earth.

Stremwynn sat and wiped his face again, and the players floated and danced around him, cooing and entreating him to get up, to speak to them, to listen to their stories.

Yes, let him live. Him only. And only this one time. The last time. Not that I will be remembered for mercy or even the attempt at mercy, not that I will be remembered for treachery or insubordination or an insult to tradition, but that I will be remembered. I have always watched the game, never played. Imagine having this grand new experience, this taste of novelty and danger, so close to the end of a life. To his, to mine.

How might I play, though? I recalled the battlefield maps in our tents on the front, wreathed in cigarette smoke so that they seemed not maps at all but a misty real world made miniature: rivers, mountains, cities. Blocks of painted wood representing thousands of lives. Yes, we made that into a game too. As if we were rolling dice and climbing ladders. It used to be the gods that played with men for their sport. Now we were the gods.

Stremwynn would never trust me. Our people had been enemies too long. And more than trust: to play along, so that he might escape rather than be swarmed by the officers, who might rise in a single seething mass and kill both him and myself.

A game inside a game, hidden. The yolk inside the shell. Outside, the serene white unblemished surface, and inside a sphere of light. Like a captured sun.

So, then. Let us play where we cannot be seen.

"Get up, Private," I called. "How can you entertain us if you will not get up?"

He glanced up, teeth bared: but at least he looked instead of ignoring me. That was, I thought, an opening move: a move and countermove. Click-clack across colored squares but everything still in its ranks for now.

What time remained? My role was to run down the clock; neither of us knew to a nicety when it would strike, and so to take out my pocket watch looked suspicious. The officers would see that, would wonder why I did it.

"Now supposing we did not place your remains in the Royal Cemetery," I called. "Would you like a burial of more majesty or less? Since you think we are so obsessed with appearances." Mezhi laughed, delighted, like a child anticipating a pummeling at a shadow puppet show. "Not in the ocean. Don't your people think it a great sacrilege to have no body? To be eaten by fish?"

A nudge. Cjesev passed me a note: *But then they do not think it is a great sacrilege to eat fish in turn! What hypocrites!*

I said, "Well, let's place your body in a glass tank in the square, and put some fish in it; and then we will eat the fish in turn." A roar of laughter behind me. "No? Perhaps a natural monument would be better? It would save us hiring a sculptor. They are very expensive, you know, the good ones. Or what about Saint Bontur's Steps?"

"Oh, those are lovely," someone said approvingly. "I shagged a milkmaid there once."

"Silence!" I barked. "Rules!" They chuckled; someone tossed a crumpled ball of paper at me and missed.

Stremwynn glared at me, but not, I thought, with comprehension.

"Don't listen to them," I said.

"I've never been there," he said, ducking a passing gear. "That's a dangerous place. There's spirits in it."

"Dangerous! Surely not for you, with your reflexes. And anyway it is perfectly natural. A simple distribution of columnar basalt, divided over many years by flowing water. Nothing mythical about it whatsoever. No? We could bury you at the top, where the water is still."

Stremwynn got up, moving again amongst the players. Very obviously ignoring me: his back tight with anger, every knob on his spine showing like a fist.

"What about a mausoleum?" I said. "We have grand ones, don't we, gentlemen? We put a lot of craftsmanship into it." I paused, as if trying to recall names and places, which in fact I was, but I wanted it also to look theatrical, even gloating. *See how rich we are*, the others would think; *see how rich and powerful and civilized and ancient we are.*

I thought: Do you think, boy, we are decadent? Do you know what that word means? Not luxurious, though it has taken on that meaning. It means *decayed*.

"Now, compare one of our finest, for the military genius who defended us from the Ustukin barbarians. A grand thing of purest white marble, in Kruend. Hmm?

You haven't visited there either, have you, even though it's near the border. Your side calls it the Tower of Ethenrien. Or no, that's not right, is it? Your silly, twisty language."

His shoulders stiffened minutely; I hoped the others had missed it, or taken it to mean that he had been baited successfully by mocking his mother tongue. They did indeed have a white marble memorial to a war hero, but it was not in Kruend, and he was named Yaratrian, not Ethenrien.

The officers would not know that. Indeed, they were laughing again, as the boy swung around and gave me the full force of his gaze. Ethenrien starred in a fairytale I had read as a child: framed for a terrible crime by his evil uncle, Ethen had been enchanted to walk an endless staircase for the rest of his life, never reaching the top. When his selfless mother offered to take his place, Ethen slew his uncle and carried his mother, near-dead of exhaustion, to the top of the staircase, which led to a magical land of freedom and treasure.

It was an obscure little story, originating in the boy's province; I had been sure he would know it. Hope flared in me for a moment, unseen, giving little warmth.

"You mock everything about us," the boy hissed. "You even mock how we speak. You are empty inside, you have no souls. We are not lesser than you. We are not animals."

"Oh, of course not."

All right, his face said before he turned back to the players. *Let's play.*

He said, "You'll tell your people I cried and begged for my life and shit my pants with fear. And the entire world will say: *They are insane and they are liars too.*"

"The entire world," I said, "will keep its mouth shut if it knows what's good for it."

Now. How to give him the signal? He too would be wondering. Up on a high, small gear, he was surrounded by a dozen or so players who had settled cozily as roosting birds, and he was feeling their wrists.

Death has a heart that beats, said the next note, the ink smeared and in an unrecognizable hand, suggesting it came from a back row. *But how clever he is to think of it! The last one did not, I am sure.*

Blast it. What other fairy tales might I use? No, I couldn't do it twice. And he was too young to know anything of much use, wasn't he. One day long ago he had been taught: *The world is round, it spins to orbit a star.* And then what must have felt like minutes later, he had been buttoned into a scratchy uniform and told: *Go kill.*

Take lives.

Do not give them back.

"Have you killed many people, Private Stremwynn?"

"What do you care, you sick bastard? Do you want to know so you can jack off to it later?"

Ah, play the game, boy; good. Murmurs behind me, still approving. Not suspicious. Or were they? It is so hard to get actionable information from a murmur.

"I certainly think you should tell me," I said.

"A *million*," he sang, holding the final note for several seconds; the hair rose stiffly on my nape. "*Ten* million. I killed every single enemy I saw. Every one of you bastards. I killed bastards I didn't even *see*. The massacre at Upper Quaril? That was me. I did it with my mind."

"Amazing! How merciful that you have chosen not to kill us all with your mind at this precise moment."

Mezhi honked with laughter, and it rippled out in waves like a stone tossed into a pond. Good. So they too, I thought suddenly, were part of the game. And they did not even know they were playing. Now we all play together, so it is like a dance.

But will the one who does not play come to watch our game? Does it cheer for a side?

"Perhaps I did," he said. He stooped with boneless grace, seized a fallen feather, tucked it into the soft black fluff behind his ear, small and red, like a cut. "And you are watching this now from Hell."

"O, a prize, a prize," sighed a lithe young woman in a military outfit from a hundred years ago, all gold braid and navy wool. "Give it, please, and I shall trade it to the Watchers of the Woods for a wish." She reached for the red feather, and Stremwynn half-instinctively danced away, losing his hat at once into the maw of two gears behind him.

I nearly cursed. The gears aligned for so brief a space, I could not let Stremwynn miss it.

He awaited a signal he could trust, still half-believing (or fully believing: let us not lie to ourselves) that I would betray him. Because I had told him the game could not be won; because he could not fathom why I had begun a second game. I did not know, entirely, myself. His death would not end the war, nor would his life. We would still be a laughingstock, just as he said. They would still be heroic martyrs. Tomorrow, more birds would be singing than today, and there would be a few more minutes of daylight.

"Now, Stremwynn—"

"Go fuck yourself."

The slightest of edges in his voice. Anger, but also impatience, if you were listening for it. My heart began to hammer.

Neither of us would win. Death was the better player: experienced, canny, full of tricks and wily endgames, impossible to deceive on the board. We would both lose. Not him. Not me.

How to make a signal he would see through the crowd of masks and ribbons, feathers and jewelry, and could not be seen from behind me? And supposing he was not looking at me at the crucial moment. I could not speak a clue of any kind; above all we wish to cheat without being caught.

"I meant to ask only about your epitaph. There isn't much room on a gravestone," I said. Sweat beaded on my brow, trickled down into my beard.

"Shut up. I am trying to talk to these people."

"Now the others, they got a mass grave," I said expansively. "It's more economical. We thought about burning them, but that whole area of the city is on fire anyway. Thanks to you. Or as you'd say, thanks to us."

"Shut up."

"Now, it's about time your people learned there are no rules in war. I'm not angry, truly. Look at our hero Minndahl's campaign back in 1357," I said. "You don't know that one. Little coalminer, hmm? A clever gambit."

"I don't *care*, nobody cares about your colonies. Why can't you people just stay where you are? Why do you have to leave *your* home and smash up or steal *everybody else's*?" Stremwynn shouted. "Why can't you *stop* when you know that everybody *hates* you?"

In the low and flickering light, this light of operas, of theatre, of magic (of murder), I could not be entirely sure of what I had seen on his face. Minndahl had successfully invaded not merely by the unexpected approach from the sea cliffs, but by staging a diversion at a distant village the night before, luring the garrison out to defend the civilians.

They will try to divert you at the crucial moment, I had meant to say. *Pay attention to me, not the diversion.*

Maybe, his slight nod had said; or had he only raised his chin and not lowered it? His skin gleamed like an ancient helmet in a museum. Dripping metal. *I am the warrior*, his face said. *Not you.*

The steps of the players had taken on a ritualized cadence, apparently random; but I spotted it at once. Randomness itself is a pattern that draws attention. Stremwynn would not be able to see that. The players harried him, threatened him, stepped close to his face, vied for his favor, nudging each other aside. Twirled away behind him so he glanced at their steps.

The gears turned. Turned. Clicked. He fell down one level. Another. *Don't let them distract you, boy. Watch me. Watch me.*

Click.

Click.

Click.

There.

Arms still crossed across my chest, I turned the whiteness of my palm to him, twice, three times, silently. Had he seen it? No? No. Dear Gods, and the seconds dribbling away like water.

Wait.

Stremwynn fought free, crying, "What did you call me? I've emptied a man's guts for less than that!" and looked up.

Time paused: hung frozen and crystalline as if suspended in a tear. And then he was in motion, trailing sweat in golden droplets, arms pumping. The players' hands fell away from him and went to their eyes as if they could not stand to look.

In long graceful leaps he took the staircase, heedless of the roars of consternation and surprise behind me. At the top he hesitated; I opened my mouth to cry *Jump!* but held it down.

He leapt, arms out.

And hit the invisible sill, and scrabbled at the light wooden latch, and had almost gotten it loose when Death revealed herself.

For a moment I was a child again, fallen in the river and caught in an eddy, spinning trapped in the cold transparent water.

Death was taller than the boy, taller than me; and she wore a black mask from brow to chin and her hair was dark without being the color of dark hair; it was the void filled with stars, and constellations glinted as it coursed down her back, the Serpent, the Scorpion, the Archivist, the Twins.

With queenly step she left the edge of her gear and rose effortlessly toward Stremwynn, her gown billowing like thunderheads at sunset, weightless gold, lifted by invisible breath, and in this furious silent cloud of storm and light she seized the boy and brought him down to the stone.

Before I could react she had dragged me up as well, one terrifying unseen burst of motion, knocking away the guards. When everything stopped moving I looked up cautiously: Stremwynn fought to free his arm and she gave him no notice, and her grip did not loosen. His teeth and his staring eyes shone in the darkness like bone.

She unclasped her mask and tossed it clatteringly aside, where the other players danced away from it like a live coal. And they were wise to do so, as I glanced only once at the place where a face should have been, and looked away.

Over the roar and hiss of my heart she spoke, and Stremwynn stopped struggling and looked down at me.

"Pardon me, lady," I said, hating how my voice trembled. "Did you address me?"

Explain yourself, Vessough. Before these so-called persons. I want them to witness it.

"Witness what?"

How you have cheated the game.

"I did nothing, lady. You know the rules as well as I. If the criminal can climb to freedom, then he may go. Which, I admit, has never happened; but the entire structure is built to enable it. We made it so."

It has never happened because the entire structure is built for it to be unnoticeable when it happens. You told him somehow, you are complicit, Vessough. Of all people.

"I deny and forswear it. I will swear upon anything you ask."

I do not ask. I ask nothing of human creatures, for there is nothing I cannot take at my whim. But this is not whim. He is mine. Belongs to me. And now we shall go.

Where she goes no one can follow, and the players were already parting to make a path, what indeed would

I have sworn upon? What in my life do I still hold holy? Nothing, no one, no gods, no memories. "Wait!"

She turned, swinging Stremwynn lightly, like a parasol. The dress stormed around her, the gold of new coins, blacker in its folds and shadows than void, something burning there, listening. On her back four great wings were unfolding, their edges lit faintly in blue and sharper than broken glass.

Nothing is holy and nothing has my faith except this: wings designed not for flight but to deliver pain to soft things. To make them bleed.

"I offer myself in his place," I said.

She said nothing.

"Let him go. Are you so attached to winning a rigged game? Or are you so attached to him? Eventually you will see him again. Perhaps minutes from now. A mob may tear him apart. A bomb may destroy him. It's war. Take me instead. He won his freedom."

The players did not move. Stremwynn did not move. The officers rose from their seats; I heard the scraping of shoes.

Death, too, did not move. And then she began to laugh, until the laughter vanished under a storm of sound as the bell struck to signal the end. Three times it rang, unmeasured tons of chipped and pitted iron, and all the world became noise, and we were washed in it, crushed by it, reduced to motes.

When it was over, my hearing returned to discover Death still laughing. The gears were still and the clock spring was entirely unwound, the great copper bulk resting lightly on its ratchet.

I rose, scraping my palms on the stone. My bones still resounded to the bell; my mouth had filled with blood. I swallowed it rather than spit at Death's feet. Her shoes looked very expensive.

I will not take you, she said. *I do not want you. But never before has the offer been made, and you have given me much mirth for making it.*

She released Stremwynn and pushed him toward me. Then Death and her billowing gown vanished into a slit cut in the air, a dainty action of one swift wing. Its light left a similar scratch on my eyes no matter where I looked, violet-blue and burning.

Stremwynn limped toward me, making for the edge of the stone support. I stopped him with a hand on his sweat-dampened shoulder.

"No. There is a door behind the spring. You will find the key to it around the neck of the lieutenant there, him on the floor. If you go past these men they will kill you. Death never flies far. You played well."

"And you?"

"Go. In a moment they will remember themselves."

The players did not stop him; the lieutenant only moaned and pawed weakly at the boy's big hands effortlessly breaking the thin chain. Then he paused, the fool, to uncouple the shackled prisoners on the spring's winding-handle, and rushed them out ahead of him.

Firelight no longer danced on the stone walls. The long light of dawn was tentative, greyish-blue, then lavender, then crimson. In silence I climbed down, and the others surrounded me, Mezhi, Cjesev, others I did not know, and they did not touch me, perhaps because Death had too recently done so and her powers lingered, perhaps for other reasons. Their hands hovered.

"Explain yourself," said Cjesev, pressing his pistol to my back. I ignored the crawling of my spine as it attempted to flee, and put on a bland smile.

"I don't know what you're talking about," I said. "You all seem to be very excited, gentlemen, over nothing whatsoever."

"What happened?" Mezhi's eyes were bloodshot, the sockets blackened, as if he had been struck across the bridge of the nose.

"I would say you seem to be having a reaction to something," I said.

"Move. We will get to the truth of this."

We emerged into a cool, smoky sunrise. Long shadows crossed my own and I looked up. On the far side of the river, Stremwynn rose clumsily from a trap door, his light uniform smeared with soot and dirt, scattering the other prisoners ahead of him.

He stared at me. Between us the river scraped and walked, walked and scraped. Mud and ash and blood. How long till it ran clear again? I would not be alive on that day.

I raised a hand to the boy, held it up long enough to ensure he saw. Noticing what I had never seen: scratches from the broken ends of ribs. A man reaches into another man and lifts out a heart, and at the end of his life his atrocities are scribbled onto his hands for anyone to read.

After a moment, Stremwynn waved back. And then he was gone, running low between the broken buildings, vanishing into the smoke.

ACKNOWLEDGMENTS

As always I would like to thank my extraordinarily patient agent Michael Curry, who somehow manages to not say "Oh no, not another novella" every time. I would have slipped quietly out of publishing and into the sea by now if I did not write everything with the warm and secure knowledge that he believes in me and my books. I would also like to thank my brilliant editor E. Catherine Tobler for understanding these stories and helping to lift them to the heights I had in my head and never quite got onto the page. I would also like to thank Sean Markey for inviting me to become part of the Psychopomp team, and for keeping me in the loop about his indefatigable efforts to bring this book to readers. My friend Jennifer R. Donohue was the catalyst for these stories—if I did not have someone to throw all my weird ideas at, these ones would have died on the vine. I am also grateful to our copyeditor, Josephine Stewart, and our cover artist John G. Reinhart.

Prish had always been the kind of radish who knew what she was about. Maybe that was why she hadn't noticed sooner that Alsing had grown pensive and quiet in the evenings, that she took longer than usual washing up the dinner dishes or with the mending. Prish had never minded long silences; a thoughtful pause could cultivate all manner of interesting things. Plants like herself tended to have more patience than animals. Their lives-before, rooted to the ground and always waiting for a glimpse of sun, required such a temperament. So, out in the sprawling gardens behind their cabin, with the friendly pat of rhubarb leaves on her shoulders and the idle conversation of bumblebees in her ears, it was too easy to miss the things that didn't get said, the hopes that got silently dashed, the neighborly visits that slowly dried up.

She'd noticed, of course, that no stars had fallen for a while. Hard to miss that their little cabin deep in the wood hadn't welcomed any newly starstruck guests. The last such had been an elderly squirrel, his dark eyes suspicious of Alsing—a fox, herself—as she offered him clothes to fit his newly human-like form (she had long experience sewing trousers with a comfortable hole in the place where a tail should emerge). He'd stayed with them for two weeks, until his two-legged tottering grew steady and confident, until he had learned his way around cutlery and shirt-buttons and even (briefly and not entirely successfully) Alsing's bicycle. Then they'd waved him off as he set out for the city, glancing back toward the cabin on every fourth or fifth step.

And not a soul since. They still sat out on the cabin's little porch each evening, with cups of iced tea in the summer and steaming mugs of mulled wine in winter, and watched the skies. Sometimes a star would streak across the sky, but it always disappeared somewhere far behind the horizon, without the telltale flare of light to herald a new-made starstruck's arrival in the world. "Looks like another quiet night," Prish would say, when her eyes grew weary and her long leafy hair wilted for want of sleep. She and Alsing hadn't yet lived in here the cabin long enough to have grown old together, but they weren't young anymore, either. "Maybe tomorrow."

"Maybe tomorrow," Alsing always agreed, and it was easy enough not to worry about the extra time she took gathering herself up out of the rocking chair, the restless flick of her ears. She was forever flicking her ears, anyway, when she hadn't yet had her morning cup of coffee or when Prish tracked dirt from the gardens into the kitchen or when she got too busy after that morning cup of coffee to take just one blasted minute to visit the outhouse, for goodness' sake.

So one evening, in the early autumn, when Prish draped a faded quilt over her wife's shoulders and kissed her cheek and invited her out to the porch, she was taken aback when Alsing said no, and burst into smothered, hiccupping sobs.

Prish maneuvered Alsing to the sofa, the same one that she'd found on the side of the street in the city twenty years ago, before they'd met. Alsing had sewn slipcovers for the arms of the sofa, to hide the worn spots and a worrying stain, and she picked at one of these now with the tip of one claw. Tea was made. Hugs were offered. A clean handkerchief was procured, and then, a second.

"It's your starday," she told Prish, with another damp honk into the much-abused handkerchief.

Prish filed this information away thoughtlessly in the coat pockets of her mind, where it would slip out again sooner or later when she rooted around there for the symptoms of grot-root in tomatoes or the last place she'd seen the farmer's almanac. She marked Alsing's starday yearly with alacrity, and with a massive bouquet of all their favorite flowers (it helped that Alsing's starday fell at the end of May). Celebrating Prish's own starday had never offered her much interest; to her it had always been a day like any other, and she'd long discouraged Alsing from making her desired fuss about it. And anyway, during the harvest season, there was plenty else to do, in the gardens and in the kitchen, besides nibble on cake; every other weekend she also hitched the cart to the back of a bicycle to take their extra provisions into the city of Eltomel, to deliver to the regular customers with whom they had arrangements.

Besides, her original starday hadn't been that big of an event to begin with. Certainly nothing as traumatic or dramatic as Alsing's. There had been a flash of light, accompanied by a flash of existence, and she'd pulled herself the rest of the way out of the soil of a small farm in the Lowland Downs. Starstruck ages didn't match up exactly to those of their human counterparts, but she would have been a young woman, built stout and sturdy in a human-like shape with knotted, twisted stems and roots in place of flesh, with clumps of dirt still clinging to the tiny hairs on her arms and legs and feet. She'd gone up to the farmhouse and knocked on the door, where a human farmer had emerged in a nightshirt and a pair of muddy boots. He'd studied her for a moment, and then yawned enormously. "Martha Ann!" he'd called over his shoulder, without quite waiting for the yawn to wrap up. "One of the watermelon radishes went and got starstruck. Fetch me down a pair of your old overalls, will you?"

And so Prish had gotten dressed, been cooked a midnight dinner of scrambled eggs and uncured bacon, and shooed off to sleep on a pile of old quilts by the old man and his daughter. When Prish woke up in the morning, the farmer handed her a basket and asked how she felt about chickens. She hadn't been sure, just then, but she'd been willing to find out. (Chickens were perfectly fine, it turned out. She would have liked to keep a henhouse at the cabin, too, but Alsing said the temptation was too great.)

Waiting for Alsing to elaborate on the importance of her starday proved fruitless. Prish stroked the back of her hand, careful to follow the grain of the fur. "I'm not sure I understand, Whiskers. I don't think you're upset that I was starstruck in the first place?"

"Well, of course not!" Annoyance displaced some of the sadness in Alsing's voice. She sat up a little straighter on the sofa and kicked Prish lightly in the shin. "Don't be ridiculous, you mean old thing." She delivered one last final-sounding blow into the handkerchief and set it aside. "It's just that it marks a different anniversary, too.

Haven't you been counting? It's been eighteen months. A year and a half." Her head turned toward the little window that let out onto the porch. "Since the last star fell."

Prish snorted. "It can't have been that long already! Why, old Vendiero was just here in the spring, and..." She trailed off, doing the mental accounting. Not this spring, was it? This spring they'd used the little guest room as a storage space after an April storm took the roof off the shed. She felt her mouth open and close a few times, but nothing came out and nothing went in, not agreement or apologies or air. "Someone would have mentioned," she insisted stubbornly. But who? They hardly ever saw their neighbors here, as far apart as they were all spread in the Craftwood, and when she went into the city, she kept her head down and made her deliveries and came swiftly back home.

"I know. I know. You do lose track of the time, dear heart." Now it was Alsing's turn to turn their hands over, so that hers lay on top of Prish's, giving back some of the comfort she'd so recently taken. "But it has been a long, long time."

"But surely somewhere else—" Prish cut herself off again. Even in Eltomel, she couldn't remember the last time someone had ushered forward a hesitant new starstruck to meet her. Someone would have said something to her, wouldn't they? But maybe it was too strange a subject to broach. Or maybe there had been gossip that Prish had missed: half-heard conversations, idle chatter.

She couldn't make it make sense. They'd seen lights in the sky, over the last year and more. Just because none of the starstruck had arrived on their doorstep didn't mean they hadn't arrived anywhere at all. "They must be falling somewhere," she insisted stubbornly.

They both sat with that hollow insistence for a moment, waiting for a fresh idea to breathe new life into it. Waiting for it to swell with real hope. But nothing came. Like the stars, it seemed, hope had somewhere better to be. If the stars were falling, they were falling too far away for them to know about it. Too far away for lonely starstruck to find their way into Eltomel to meet her.

It was too much to contemplate what might have stoppered up the stars; what it meant that the world would be deprived of any more beings as wonderful as Alsing ever again. Prish had always been the kind of radish who knew what she was about, and what she was about fell comfortably within the fences of her garden and the walls of her house and the confines of her heart. What she had always been about, really, was Alsing.

Alsing held out the quilt to one side, and Prish squeezed in alongside her, her chin resting on Alsing's shoulder, Alsing's ear flicking restlessly against the top of her head.

There was nothing else to do then but to ask it, the only question she could think of, the one whose answer she already knew and had to hear anyway.

"What do you want to do now?" she said.

"I..." Alsing's ears stilled, flattening along the back of her head. "I don't want to be here anymore."

Prish marshaled arguments she knew would never see combat: the garden bed she'd just tucked in for a winter slumber under a thick blanket of compost, and the stalks still waiting for the first frost before they offered up one last harvest of sweet, plump sprouts. The

raspberry jungle she'd coaxed out of a few recalcitrant canes, and the bench built for two on the back porch, and the three apple trees she'd planted last year that she would never see bear fruit. The last pumpkins, still green and unfulfilled on the vine.

"Well then," Prish said briskly, sending her disappointment and disagreement to an unearned early retirement. "It only makes sense for us to go."

Starstruck by Aimee Ogden
Coming from Psychopomp, coming 2025
Join our mailing list to stay up to date on this and other exciting releases, psychopomp.com

Aimee Ogden is an American werewolf in the Netherlands. After twenty years in Wisconsin, it was finally time to trade in fried cheese curds for bitterballen and bami goreng. Aimee is the co-founder, co-publisher, and former co-editor of *Translunar Travelers Lounge,* a speculative fiction magazine devoted to fun, optimistic stories. When she's not anchored to her computer, she can be found snuggled up with her two ten-year-old burgeoning readers, biking around town, or practicing her mediocre Dutch.

ONE MESSAGE REMAINS

"*Premee Mohamed sends her readers once more unto the breach with her stunning stories and I for one am sure to follow wherever she leads the charge. The battlefield has never been more breathtaking, where the horrors of war go beyond the borders of our own world, explored with such probing, insightful prose.*"

—Clay McLeod Chapman, author of *Wake Up and Open Your Eyes*

"*Nebula award winner Mohamed delivers more science-infused, dystopian speculative fiction in this hard-hitting collection of four interlinked stories.*"

—Publisher's Weekly

"*Premee Mohamed is one of speculative fiction's greatest authors, and this collection provides further proof.*"

—Chuck Wendig

"*Premee Mohamed is one of Canada's most exciting thinkers and writers of speculative fiction. Her stories bravely go where few dare to, each employing a deftness of language and surety of form that offers a fresh experience each time.* One Message Remains *and the stories within are no exception, each tale different from the other, yet all very much quintessential Premee stories. Readers of her works, long and short both, will find much to love here.*"

—Suyi Davies Okungbowa

"*Nobody writes like Premee Mohamed, with justice on one shoulder and compassion on the other, and a pen that dances over the page. In* One Message Remains, *she draws different voices and perspectives to the fore like a conductor of a small and beautifully crafted symphony, in a minor key.*"

—Kate Heartfield, Aurora Award winner and author of *The Tapestry of Time*

"*Mohamed has given us an incisive collection that unflinchingly dissects the brutal clockwork mechanism behind colonialism and the very real, flesh and blood people who are caught within its cogs. Beautifully penned, insightful and honest in it's portrayal of resistance, this is exactly the brave kind of anticolonial work we need now more than ever.*"

—Suzan Palumbo author of *Countess* and *Skin Thief Stories*

"Gallows creak, the perished whisper, and death herself watches from the audience. On stages, on the run, and in graves, people try to find ways of resisting the oppression that has controlled them for so long. A beautiful collection of stories with prose that sings until your very bones resonate with their melody."

—Steve Toase, author of *Dirt Upon My Skin* and *To Drown in Dark Water*

"An established master of short fiction, Mohamed brings her typical clarity and assurance to a new—but desperately familiar—world haunted by violence, empire, ghosts, and devils. These are simply some of the most human and humane stories I've ever read."

—Alix E. Harrow, Hugo-Award Winner and *New York Times* Bestselling author

THE BUTCHER OF THE FOREST

"Written with the deft hands of a master, this is a tale for anyone who loves an ancient cursed forest (including us, Team Premee), a take-no-shit protagonist (also us), and exciting, inventive magic (you guessed it—we love that shit)."

—*Reactor* Magazine

"Heart-breaking and fear-striking, this book will catch you up in its claws and wring you out, all in the best possible way!"

—The Library Ladies

THE RIDER, THE RIDE, THE RICH MAN'S WIFE

"Wonderfully textured, and both chilling and heartening in equal measure."

—Mike Brooks, author of The God-King Chronicles

"A beautiful fever-dream of a story, about family, friendship, and fear."

—Laura Anne Gilman, award-winning author of the Devil's West series